M000119107

SHELTER

A HEROES OF BIG SKY NOVEL

KRISTEN PROBY

AMPERSAND PUBLISHING, INC.

Shelter
A Heroes of Big Sky Novel
By
Kristen Proby

SHELTER

A Big Sky Novel - Heroes of Big Sky

Kristen Proby

Copyright © 2021 by Kristen Proby

All Rights Reserved. This book may not be reproduced, scanned, or distributed in any printed or electronic form without permission from the author. Please do not participate in or encourage piracy of copyrighted materials in violation of the author's rights. All characters and storylines are the property of the author and your support and respect are appreciated. The characters and events portrayed in this book are fictitious. Any similarity to real persons, living or dead, is coincidental and not intended by the author.

Cover Design: By Hang Le

Cover Image by Wander Aguiar Photography

Published by Ampersand Publishing, Inc.

Paperback ISBN: 978-1-63350-112-6

This is for Seth.
For the little boy who tugged at my heartstrings all those years ago.
And for the man he's become.

PROLOGUE

~SETH~

"*I*f the kid wasn't in the car, I'd give you the best blowjob of your life right now," my mom says to her boyfriend and then scowls at me as I sit in the back seat. We've driven all the way from Texas to Montana in this horrible car with the smell of his cigarettes, and they don't stop when I tell them I have to go to the bathroom.

"He'll be gone soon," he says and grabs her boob.

My stomach feels queasy. I don't like it when she lets men touch her like that in front of me.

At least, it's not as bad as what she lets them do *to* me. As long as they get to touch her, they leave me alone.

I hope she leaves me and never comes back.

The road to the ranch is bumpy, and I have to pee so bad, I'm afraid I'll go in my pants. But I don't say

1

anything because we're almost there, and then I won't have to be with my mom anymore.

I hope. I hope that Gram and Gramps let me stay. What if they don't?

My stomach is even queasier when I think about that, so I just push it away. They were always nice to me before. They let me help with the animals and gave me all the food I could eat. And, sometimes, Grandma even made pie for dessert.

"Thank God, we're here." Mom opens her car door. "Get out of the car, Seth."

I climb out and eye my grandparents warily. They're both standing on the porch. Uncle Josh is here, too, but he doesn't look happy.

Will they send me away?

Mom tosses my bag onto the ground next to me. I don't have much in there. She didn't let me take very much because she said they didn't have room in the car.

"What's this about?" Uncle Josh asks.

"Seth's your problem now," Mom replies. Her voice is hard. It's been that way for a long, long time.

I don't look up at any of them. I just stare at the ground and make circles in the gravel with my shoes.

What if they don't want me?

"Seth isn't a problem," Grandma says and rushes down the porch steps, pulling me against her. I instinctively stiffen.

No one ever touches me in a nice way. It's usually just to push me aside or give me a whoopin'.

"He is for me," Mom says. She and Uncle Josh talk about how she doesn't want me anymore because she has Cole now, and she doesn't like being a mom.

She's not good at it, anyway.

But then she starts talking about my dad, and I want to yell at her to shut her mouth. To stop talking about him.

All he ever does is leave. He doesn't even want to talk to me when he calls.

I hate him.

But I don't say anything. I just stand with Grandma and hope with all my might that I get to stay here with the animals, where it's safe. Where I can eat until my belly is full, and no one will put their hands on me if I don't want them to.

I don't even care when Mom starts screaming, throwing a fit in front of Uncle Josh and the others.

She does this all the time.

"Seth is always welcome here," Uncle Josh says, and for the first time since I can remember, I take a deep breath.

They're going to let me stay!

He walks over to my mom and stands over her. He's big. *Really* tall. And I can tell by the way her eyes get wide that she's scared of him.

Good. I want her to be scared. Like she made me feel for so long.

3

"But *you* are not. Seth will stay with us until Zack is back in the States in a few months. You are never to come back here." He gets even closer to her. "If you ever show your face here again, I'll have you arrested for trespassing, and I will ruin your pathetic life."

Mom sputters, steps back, and then gets her mad face back on again.

"Why would I ever come back here? There's nothing here I want." She doesn't even look at me before getting back into the car. They zoom away, headed for the highway.

"Oh, honey," Grandma whispers and kisses my head.

I just shrug and pull away.

I don't like being touched.

"Can I stay here, Uncle Josh?" I ask, just to make sure. Magic, my favorite horse, makes a noise, and I let my gaze flick her way.

"Of course, buddy. You always have a place here."

I want to smile. I want to jump and dance with relief. But I'm just so tired. And sore. And hungry.

So, I only nod and look down at the ground until they tell me what to do.

"Come on, Seth," my grandfather says. "Grandpa will show you to your room. You can have your dad's old room."

Anger boils up in my throat, and I shake my head, my hands balling into fists. "I don't want anything of his. I'd rather sleep in the barn."

"Okay, the spare room it is, then."

"Come on, honey, let's get you settled, and I'll fix you some lunch," Grandma says with a smile. She wraps her arm around me, and I don't pull away. It's kind of nice. And she's going to make me something to eat! My stomach growls. "We've missed you so much. There are some fish out in the creek that need to be caught, you know."

Fishing is what I like the best. Well, next to the horses. When I was here a few years ago, Uncle Josh and Dad took me fishing every day. Maybe we'll go again.

Maybe today.

Grandma takes me upstairs to my new bedroom. It has a nightlight so I won't be in the dark all the time.

I don't like the dark.

"Would you like a sandwich?" Grandma asks.

"Sure." I shrug and secretly hope I can have chips, too. I don't want to ask for them, though. Whenever I ask, Mom takes everything away.

"Let's go down to the kitchen, and you can hang out with me while I make lunch. We have potato salad and chips if you want them. And I even made a chocolate cake yesterday, if you want some dessert."

My mouth waters at the thought of all that food.

I love it here.

I hope I can stay forever.

CHAPTER 1

~SETH~

"Got one!" I smile in triumph and show the trout off to my uncle and dad, who are just about twenty yards away.

We're at the creek behind the house on the King ranch, enjoying a rare, late-summer day off with a little fishing.

It'll be good as long as they're biting.

"That's a tiny one," Uncle Josh says with a smirk, and I scowl down at the wiggling fish in my hand.

"It's not that tiny." Still, I unhook it and drop it back into the water. "Have you heard from the fish and wildlife people about the wolf problem?"

"They'll be here tomorrow morning," Josh says with a grim sigh. "This happens about every five years or so, and we end up losing a lot of calves. It pisses me off."

"I hope they can get it figured out. I'll help if I can," I offer.

I have a degree in wildlife biology, and I've been working with Glacier National Park for the last several years. I have experience. And, frankly, I have a personal stake in this.

This is King land. And I'm a King.

I plan to be here for the rest of my life.

"If you have time to meet them with us," Dad says as he casts his line, "that would be great."

"I'll make time."

This ranch and the family on it are everything to me. They saved me from the pits of hell and showed me what it is to belong somewhere. To be loved.

To feel safe.

And I'll be here for the rest of my life, taking care of our home and proving to them all that I'm worthy of it.

"How is Melinda?" Uncle Josh asks with a grin.

"Ah, well." I shrug and pull in my line, frowning when I see that the worm is gone, but there's no fish in its place. Reaching for fresh bait, I answer. "She started talking about babies."

Dad's head whips around to mine. "You've dated for what? Three months?"

"Two." I cast the line. "So, I had to end that one. She said I needed to figure out what I want in a relationship."

"Jesus, after two months?" Josh demands and then shakes his head.

"Well, to be fair, you knew within two months that you loved Aunt Cara."

"I knew the minute I laid eyes on her." Josh winks at me. "But it doesn't always happen like that."

"Yeah, Melinda was a little clingy. And it didn't exactly break my heart when I broke it off, so it clearly wasn't meant to be."

"You're young," Dad says with a shrug.

"What do you say we drink beer and watch football tonight?" Josh asks.

"Can't. I'm going out with Gage to shoot some pool."

"How's Gage?"

"I think he's doing well. He's been busy. Haven't talked to him much lately, but I'll catch up with him later. Cara's making spaghetti for dinner, and I'm sticking around for it."

Josh's phone rings.

"Speak of the devil," he mutters and answers the phone. "Hey, Carolina. What?"

He frowns and then hides a laugh behind his hand.

"I understand. Well, I'd like to keep my balls, so we'll be right there. We're coming. Yes, we'll hurry."

He hangs up and then lets the laugh go.

"What's up?" Dad asks.

"She found a mouse." We all reel in our lines and make our way up the small hill, walking through the woods toward the house. "It's the second one this week."

"Wonder where they're coming in from," I mumble.

"I was supposed to look around, but I forgot," Josh

9

says. "You can bet your ass that I won't forget now. She's losing her damn mind."

"Jillian would burn the place to the ground," Dad says, referring to the woman who raised me.

"Cara threatened it."

We climb the back steps and walk into the newly renovated house, stopping short at the scene before us.

My aunt Cara, a woman who is always calm and collected, is sitting on the dining room table, holding a shotgun.

Her blue eyes look a little crazy.

"Uh, babe?" Josh steps forward and gingerly takes the firearm from her. "You can't shoot a mouse with a shotgun."

"Says who?" she demands. "You didn't see the size of the son of a bitch. It was bigger than a tomcat."

Given that we have several toms out in the barn, she would know.

Of course, there are no mice in the barn—because we have the cats.

"Where did it go?" I ask.

"Under the couch," she says and shudders. "It laughed at me."

I smirk but school my features immediately when she narrows her eyes at me.

Pissing off the *other* woman who raised me is not something I ever want to do.

"We'll find it," I promise her. "Get a bowl from the kitchen."

"You're *not* putting that monster in one of my bowls," she says, shaking her head. "That's disgusting. We *eat* out of those bowls."

"Don't you have an old one that we can throw away after we relocate the mouse?"

"Relocate?" She tilts her head and stares at me like I'm crazy. "That sucker doesn't get to *relocate*. I want it dead. I want its whole family *dead*."

"She's really homicidal," I mutter to my uncle.

"Babe, why don't you go over to the big house and hang out with Jillian while we take care of this?"

"I'm not getting off this table."

Josh just smiles gently at his wife and lifts her into his arms, grabbing her purse as he carries her out the front door.

"They're still really mushy, even after all this time."

"Are you saying I'm not mushy with your mom?" Dad asks.

"No, you are. It's gross."

Dad laughs, and then we see the offending rodent run across the living room.

"Shit, that *is* a big sucker," I say in surprise. "I need something to pick it up with."

Josh hurries back inside and turns to my dad. "Okay, she's headed over to your place. Holy shit, is that it?"

"Yeah. It's a monster. She's right. I need something to hold it in. What about Tupperware?"

"We have something," Josh says and rummages

11

through the kitchen, returning with an old to-go container that clearly held spaghetti sauce at some point given the red stain.

"Perfect. Okay, we have to corner it."

The three of us work as a team, laughing as the mouse darts around the room. Finally, I jump onto my belly and stretch to cover it with the container.

"Success!" I grin as I slide the lid under it and secure it in place. "I need to go let it go before it suffocates."

"Don't tell Cara that we let it live," Dad suggests.

"Oh, I won't. Trust me. Now, let's figure out how they're making their way inside."

I walk out to the field behind the house, close to the woods that lead to the river, and let it go.

"Now, don't come back. Be smart. Stay out here."

When I return to the house, Josh is pulling a piece of duct tape off the roll.

"Find it?" I ask.

"Yep. Looks like there's a hole under the sink that didn't get repaired correctly during the remodel. We'll keep them out with this for now, and I'll call the contractor to come back and do this correctly."

"I'm sure Aunt Cara will be relieved that you solved the case." I check the time. "I'm going to go get some work done before dinner."

My little house is new and sits on two acres, less than half a mile from the house I grew up in. Josh and Dad gave me the land as a gift for my twenty-fifth birthday a couple of years ago, and I got to work building my place.

It's a farmhouse-style ranch house with three bedrooms and two bathrooms. It has plenty of room, especially given I don't plan on it being more than just me living here.

I'm not going to have kids. After the early childhood I had, I shudder to think what kind of parent I'd make.

Hell, I don't even plan to get *married.*

This house is perfect for a life-long bachelor.

I kick off my fishing boots, strip out of my sweaty T-shirt, and make a beeline for the shower.

"Out of practice," Gage says with a laugh when I miss the pocket.

"I don't exactly have time to work on my pool game," I remind him as I reach for my beer and watch him circle the table. "How's it going with your client? Is Tate starting to feel better?"

Gage frowns and then nods slowly. "It's a damn slow process. I've been working with her for a while now, but she's standing."

"By herself?"

Tate Donovan, Aunt Cara's cousin, had a massive stroke last year. At just over thirty, it was a complete shock to everyone. The stroke was severe enough that it put her in a wheelchair, and she's had to go through many months of different therapies.

Gage is back from the Army and took the job of helping Tate regain the use of her legs and find her balance.

"By herself," he confirms. "But I found out she's been doing too much on her own and fell the other day. Damn stubborn woman."

I cock my head to the side, watching my friend. "Is something going on with you two besides the working relationship?"

"No." He sips his beer. "She drives me nuts. Hard-headed, that's what she is."

"And you're the picture of grace and patience. Not to mention flexibility."

"Fuck you."

I laugh, but then I'm pushed forward when someone stumbles into me from behind.

"Oh, God, I'm sorry."

I turn, glance down, and feel my heart lurch.

Big, blue eyes.

No, not blue.

Lavender.

"I think I spilled beer on your shoes." The petite woman with the purple eyes cringes and reaches for a pile of napkins. "I'm *never* this clumsy. I tripped on that barstool. I'm really sorry. I'll pay for your shoes if you want."

"It's fine." I touch her shoulder before she leans over to dab at my feet. "Really, it's fine."

She blows out a breath, and my dick twitches at the sight of those plump lips.

Jesus, the woman is *beautiful.*

"You're not from here," I say and gesture for her to sit on the stool.

"How do you know that?"

"Because I'd remember that gorgeous face."

A smile flirts with her lips, and a single dimple creases in her right cheek. "No. I'm just in town for a couple of weeks."

Before she can turn and walk away, I think fast. I don't know what it is about this girl, but I want to hang out with her. Get to know her a bit.

Kiss those delectable lips.

"Want to dance?" I ask and point to the live band up on stage.

"Oh. Uh, sure. I guess."

I take her hand in mine and wink at Gage before leading her out onto the dance floor. Her hand is dainty, but her grip is strong.

When we start to move, her body glides effortlessly. Her brown hair is up off her neck, and she's in a tank top that shows off the definition of muscle in her arms and shoulders.

She's in excellent shape.

And her jeans mold to her ass perfectly.

When one song ends and bleeds into a slow song, I pull her to me, and we move lazily around the space.

She has her nose pressed to my shoulder.

Her breasts push against my chest.

I've never been so turned on by a woman after only five minutes.

I glance up and see Gage waving at me. He's headed out.

I nod in reply.

I'll call him later.

When the song is over, and with my entire body humming, I escort her back to where I was sitting with Gage.

"You're a good dancer," she says.

"All the better for holding gorgeous women." I wink and then laugh when she just raises a brow. "Okay, that was cheesy. But it was nice to touch you."

"Are you always this forward?" she asks.

"No, actually. What's your name?"

"Remi. And you?"

"Seth." I shake her hand. Rather than letting go, I link my fingers with hers and bring them up to my mouth so I can kiss her knuckles.

She grins and doesn't pull away.

"Remi is a beautiful name."

"Thanks. So, are you from here?"

"Yes." I don't count the years that I spent with Kensie. "Where are you from?"

"Southern California, originally. I've been doing

some traveling, and I heard this part of the country is beautiful. So far, they're right."

"It's a little late in the season."

It's mid-September. Most of the summer activities are closed for the upcoming winter.

"I like to travel when fewer people are around. And I lucked out because the weather has been great. I'm living the van life, and Montana is perfect for it."

She frowns as if she just realized that she shouldn't tell a stranger that she's living in a van.

God, I want to kiss her.

"We could get snow by the weekend."

She laughs and shakes her head. "Yeah, right. It's September."

"In Montana," I remind her. "Could happen."

"How do you know?" Her eyes narrow, and she leans on the tall table to her right. "Are you a weatherman?"

"No." I laugh and have to curb the impulse to reach out and touch her. "I'm a ranger up in the park, and we've seen snow earlier than this up there. The weather reports are calling for a chance of snow in the higher altitudes."

"But, it's just a *chance.* It probably won't." She shrugs and frowns at her drink. "I'm not drinking this. I left it alone for too long."

"Good call. I'll go get us some fresh drinks. Do you want the same beer?"

"That would be great."

"You stay here. I'm not done with you yet." I point at her, grin and make my way to the bar. The line is long, and by the time I get the two bottles, it's been at least ten minutes since I walked away from Remi.

When I return to our seats, they're empty.

But on the small table is a note.

Seth-

Sorry. I just can't.

R

I take a swig of the beer and swear under my breath.

Just my luck. The first woman I've been truly interested in in a long time, and she ghosts me.

I set the bottles on the high-top and rack the balls on the table.

If I can't flirt with a beautiful woman, I might as well work on my pool game so I can kick Gage's ass the next time I see him.

CHAPTER 2

~REMI~

*C*unningham Falls, Montana isn't what I expected it to be when I set off in my van two months ago. I put Los Angeles in my rearview, excited for some new adventures all on my own and without a camera crew in my face.

And I looked forward to coming to northwest Montana the most, but I thought I'd be in the boonies. That there may not be electricity everywhere and that people would ride on horses way more than I've seen in the four days I've been in town. There *are* plenty of mountains that look like a traveler's postcard and wide-open spaces, though. I can't stop staring at the views.

But while I don't have the best cell service, that seems to be the only inconvenience I've found so far. Given that I'd rather never see social media again in my life, I'm not sad about it.

Surprisingly, this little mountain town is modern with all of the conveniences I love in the city, including a gorgeous yoga studio, plenty of delicious restaurants, and a farmer's market that had me longing for my gourmet kitchen in my apartment in California.

My former apartment, that is.

I gave that up, along with my car and most of my belongings so I could live the travel-van life. And until I saw the produce at last night's farmer's market, I haven't regretted it at all. I have to admit, even the thought of making fresh marinara isn't enough for me to go back to my old life. I have a stove in the van, I can make it work if I really want.

Given that the busy tourist season recently ended, I found a great RV park on the outskirts of town that had room for me, and the nice owners told me I could stay for as long as I want.

Right now, I'm paying weekly.

I don't have a schedule. I don't have a *plan.*

And after so many years of tight deadlines and every minute scheduled down to the second, I like it this way.

Early mornings are my favorite time of day, no matter where I am, but it's quickly become even more so the case here in this little town. Autumn is settling in, adding a crispness to the air—especially early in the day.

The sliding door of my van is open, and I'm sipping

coffee as I listen to the birds and watch the sky turn from gray to blue.

The campground is quiet. The few others here must still be sleeping.

Today is my relaxation day. I've been driving or hiking every day for several weeks, so I decided that now is a good time just to *be*. Which isn't easy for me. I don't like sitting around. Being lazy is *not* my thing. I wish I could relax, but it always feels like I'm wasting time when I do. That I could be accomplishing something productive.

Today, I plan to ride my bike the mile into town, get breakfast, then stop at the store for some of my favorite snacks. And then, come hell or high water, I'm going to take a nap, watch a movie, and maybe even read a book.

I have the hiking guide for Glacier National Park that I bought a year ago when I first thought about this adventure, and it's probably best that I at least plan out the hike I want to take tomorrow.

So, with that decided, I drink the last of my coffee.

If I relax today, I can hike tomorrow.

It'll be my reward.

I tuck my wallet into the bag on my bike, make sure the van is locked up tight, and set off for the little deli I found on the main drag in town.

It's literally called *Little Deli*.

Cunningham Falls has a quaint downtown that's about three city blocks long. That's it. And it's damn adorable. I bet it looks like a Hallmark movie in the winter.

I lean my bike against a post on the sidewalk and don't even bother locking it up before stepping inside Little Deli. They serve amazing sandwiches and soups in the afternoon, but in the morning, it's my own private slice of Heaven.

"Good morning," the woman behind the counter says with a smile. "What can I get for you today?"

She's in here every day, and I'd say she's in her early forties, with just a couple of gray strands in her shoulder-length dark hair. She has kind eyes and a pretty smile.

I place my order for scones, a cheese-and-turkey-stuffed croissant, and another coffee, then sit at a table with my treats. I like to sit in the corner so I can people watch as I eat.

So far, the people here in town have been super nice. And last night, when I decided to go out for just *one* beer, I met Seth.

I sigh at the memory of that tall, handsome drink of water, who had his hands all over me and definite interest in his big, brown eyes.

He was damn tempting.

But I'm not here for that.

"Can I get you anything else, dear?"

I smile at the nice woman and shake my head. "No, thanks. This is great."

It's still early enough on this Saturday morning that

as I leave the deli and ride toward the grocery, few cars are out and about. There's a stillness in the air, contentment that feels comforting.

No, this place isn't at all what I expected, but I like it. I like it a lot.

∼

"BEAR SPRAY," I mutter and clamp the red can with the huge grizzly on the side to my belt. I have plenty of snacks in my pack, along with water, ultra-light trekking poles, extra socks, and a rain slicker rolled up at the bottom.

I went to an outdoor adventure store yesterday and picked up a survival straw to help filter water if I need it, and a fire striker in case I have to start a fire.

I definitely won't need any of the extra survival stuff. I'm way overprepared, and I don't love that I'm carrying the extra weight, but I'm also hiking alone, and it's better to be safe than sorry—even if it is only a fifteen-mile trek through the mountains. Compared to some of the hikes I've done in the past, this is an easy, eight-hour day. In and out. But according to all of my research, I'm promised some amazing views, a glacier, and hopefully some wildlife.

"Just not hungry bears," I say out loud as I lock up the van and head off for the trailhead. "Any wildlife but hungry, carnivorous ones, thanks."

The first part of the hike is all uphill. I'll gain about four thousand feet in elevation.

But that means it's all downhill on the way back when I'm starting to fatigue.

The trail is well-traveled and marked so I can just relax and enjoy.

"What a beautiful place," I say to myself. I've made it a habit of talking to myself when I hike so I don't surprise any animals. "I don't know if I've ever felt so calm. So at *peace*. Certainly not in a long, long time."

My heart rate climbs, and my breath gets choppier as I ascend deeper into the park. I'm so lost in my thoughts that it takes me a few minutes to realize that little white flakes have begun to swirl around me.

I frown and blink. "Snow? It's freaking *September*."

And then I remember what the sexy Seth said to me the other night.

We could get snow by the weekend.

"I've never been anywhere, aside from Peru, where it snows in September." I look up at the sky and sigh, then check my GPS.

I'm almost six miles in.

"I'm not turning back now," I say and keep moving forward. "I want to see this chalet that people hike up to in the summer, and I'll be damned if I don't make it farther up to the glacier. It's *Glacier* National Park, for the love of Moses. I'm going to stand on a glacier."

It's been on my bucket list for years.

The flakes start to fall faster, harder. They're big and fluffy, and I have to stop to wipe my face.

I wish I'd brought my gaiter to keep the cold droplets from falling down my neck.

Also…it's cold up here. Colder than I expected.

I'm wearing thick pants to protect my legs from thorny bushes and am in a long-sleeved shirt, but aside from my rain slicker, I don't have outerwear to protect me from a winter storm.

I stop to catch my breath and take stock of my surroundings. It's gone quiet. No birds sing. No critters skitter around in the trees.

That's a bad sign.

A bad, bad sign.

"Damn it," I mutter and rub my nose. If the map is right, I'm less than a mile from the chalet. Of course, it's closed for the season, so I can't take shelter there.

"The glacier is another couple of miles after that," I continue, just before the wind picks up and slaps me in the face with its cold, bitter hand. "Shit. I have to go back."

I turn, look at the trail that leads down, and scowl. The snow is falling so thickly now, I can't even make out the path. I know to walk downhill, but it'll be hard to move quickly if I can't see the damn route.

If I keep going to the chalet, I could hunker down against the outside of the building, but if it continues to snow—and gets colder—I could freeze.

"Maybe I can break out a window and slip inside."

I chew on my lip. I have to make up my mind, or I'll freeze to death right here, and then I *will* end up as bear food.

That's not a pleasant thought.

"You didn't listen."

I spin at the voice and goggle as Seth moves quickly up the path and through the snow.

"Are you a hallucination?"

"No, damn it. I told you we'd get snow."

"It's September," I reply, suddenly feeling immense relief that he's here. My knees threaten to buckle, and I want to cry.

"No time to argue," he says. "Are you hurt?"

"No."

"Good. Let's go."

Seth takes my hand and leads me up the path, away from the direction of my van. The pace is brutally fast, the wind merciless against my face, but I keep up with him, running on the trail that he seems to know so well.

At last, through the thick veil of snow, I see the outline of a huge building.

"We're going in!" Seth yells back at me and leads me to a door. He fiddles with some keys, and the next thing I know, he pulls me into the shelter and slams the door behind us.

It's dark inside because the place has been closed up for the winter, but Seth has a flashlight.

"There's no electricity," he says, his voice sharp in

the cold room. "No water services. But we're not in the snow."

"How did you find me?"

He turns those dark eyes on me. He looks so *mad.*

"I was patrolling the area and saw your van at the trailhead. I remembered that you said you were coming up here to hike, and I knew this storm was moving in and that you'd get caught in it, so I hiked up to get you."

"You hiked almost seven miles just to warn me about the storm?"

He blinks at me and then shakes his head. "No, I hiked almost seven miles to freaking get you *out* of this storm so you don't freeze to death, Remi. Which is exactly what was about to happen. Now, we'd better get a move on lighting a fire and getting some heat in here, or we'll meet the same fate. And I'll be damned if I go out like that."

The room we're in is a big, open space with tables and chairs set up restaurant-style. There's also a desk—I assume for visitors checking in. A huge fireplace takes up most of the far wall, where Seth is currently stacking firewood.

"I have a starter," I announce and pull my pack off my back. "I brought one with me, just in case."

He merely holds out his hand, and I pass the tool over, watching as Seth expertly lights the fire. With the flames to light the room, he switches off the flashlight to conserve its battery life.

For the first time since I saw that first flake, I take a long, deep breath.

"Thank you," I say at last.

"Do you always brush off the experts when they give you advice?" he asks and folds his arms over his chest.

"Honestly, I didn't think there was any way it would snow. It seems early in the season."

"Are you an expert on Montana, then?"

I feel my cheeks heat and turn away from him. "Look, I get it. I'm an asshole. I should have listened. And because I didn't, I almost killed myself and put you in danger, too. I'm sorry, okay? I feel foolish and irresponsible, and I'm never those things when it comes to adventuring."

He blows out a breath, pushes his hands through his hair, and licks his lips.

"Okay. Okay, I hear you. The storm is supposed to hang around for about twelve hours. We have to settle in and ride it out here. I was able to radio to the office and let the rangers there know that I was headed up here to help you. I told them I'd bring you up to the chalet and that we'd wait here until the storm passes."

"So, no one is going to panic when you don't get back today?"

"No." He takes his pack off his back and sets it next to mine. "I don't have much in here for food. I do have some water, though."

"I have some water and a few snacks," I reply. "You

don't think there's any canned food stashed away here, left over from the summer, do you?"

"I doubt it, but we'll look. They don't usually leave stuff up here because of the wildlife. There are bedrooms upstairs with lots of blankets and pillows, though. I suggest we gather some and bring them down here in front of the fire."

"Good idea. You're really good at this survivalist stuff."

"It's my job," he reminds me. "If you want to stay here by the fire, I can manage with the blankets and stuff."

"I can help."

He's so damn good-looking. I thought maybe my brain had done some fine-tuning and made my memory of him hotter than he really is. But no. He's just *hot*. He's ridiculously tall, well over six feet, and has dark brown hair, brown eyes, and sun-kissed skin. He's bundled up in cold weather gear but takes off his puffy jacket and loops it around me.

"It'll be cold up there," he says softly as I push my arms into the coat and soak in his warmth. "Bundle up in this for now."

"Thanks." I offer him a smile, and his eyes flick down to my lips before he pulls away and leads me, with the help of his flashlight and the one I found in my pack, to the staircase. I can see my breath as we climb, and he opens the first door we come to.

There's a simple queen-sized bed. Blankets and a

quilt are folded and lying on the simple mattress, covered in plastic.

I grab the blankets and pillows, plastic and all, and hurry down to set them in front of the fire, then hurry back up for more.

"You take these, and I'll be right down," Seth says, passing me more linens. I turn and immediately follow directions. My fingers and toes are damn cold, and I'd like to huddle by the fire to warm up.

Once I reach the fireplace, I turn back to the stairs and see Seth coming down with a mattress on his broad back.

"Holy shit, Seth."

"This will be more comfortable," he says and drops the mattress about six feet from the fire. "Better than a hard floor, anyway."

Before I can say anything, he marches away again and grabs a couple of chairs, bringing them to our makeshift living room before setting them down.

"In case you don't want to sit on the floor," he says and then hurries off once more. I scurry along after him, wondering where he's going.

"You move really fast for a big guy," I inform him as I follow him into the kitchen.

"Yeah, well, it's move around or be cold. And I don't like to be cold." He opens cupboards, but they're all empty. He stomps over to a pantry and lets out a long, low whistle.

"Jackpot," I whisper.

Cans of vegetables, tuna, and other staples line the shelves. There are even some granola bars, candy bars, and soups.

"I guess they haven't been up yet to take all of this down," Seth says. "Looks like we won't starve."

"I mean, if we're only stuck up here for twelve hours, we definitely won't starve, Seth. I have jerky and protein bars and stuff."

"The *storm* is supposed to last that long," he reminds me. "It'll pass in the middle of the night. Once it does, there will be up to two feet of snow. It's going to take a while for us to get out of here. So, you can bet your pretty little ass that I'll be taking some of this food with us."

"I really messed up, didn't I?"

"Well, on a scale of one to ten—one being a tiny little thing and ten being the end of the world..." He sighs and looks up like he's thinking it over. "I'd give this about a nine-point-five."

"Wow. That's pretty bad."

"If it was a ten, you'd be dead."

He grabs a few things off the shelf, and then we hurry back to the fire, which already needs another log.

I spread the blankets across the mattress, then take off my shoes and sit on the bedding, facing the fire.

We can hear the wind whipping around outside, and something slams against the outside of the building, startling me.

"Probably just a tree," Seth mutters as he takes a bite

31

of a candy bar. "Well, I suppose since we'll be holed up here together for the next couple dozen hours or so, we should get to know each other better."

He takes another bite.

"Why were you so hell-bent on coming up here today?"

I scratch my chin and look him in the eyes. "Because someone once told me that I couldn't. And that pissed me off."

CHAPTER 3

~SETH~

I still want to paddle her ass for putting us both in this situation. The entire hike up, every single mile, I cursed her for being stubborn and potentially putting herself in danger.

When the snow started to fall, my heart lodged itself squarely in my throat.

I *know* how dangerous these mountains can be. They're merciless. I've been on more search and rescue missions, that all ended badly, than I care to count.

And now that the adrenaline has died down, and we're settled in front of the fire, safely riding out the storm, I could still choke her.

But she apologized, and I know she feels foolish. I just hope she never tries anything stupid like this again.

Not that it's any of my business what she does once she leaves my park.

The firelight dances on her skin, and her dark hair

looks black in the dimness of the room behind her. Her throat works as she swallows some water, and I want to lean in and kiss her there.

Jesus, I've thought of little else since I saw her in the bar the other night.

And I only know her first name.

"So, who was the asshole?" I ask to distract myself from the long line of that neck.

"Huh?" Her gaze whips over to mine in confusion.

"The jerk who told you that you couldn't climb this mountain."

She shrugs a shoulder and turns back to the fire. "Someone I used to know a long time ago. I've always loved hiking, biking, rafting. You name it. If it's an outdoor activity, I want to do it. It's my jam. And this guy I dated once must have been intimidated by that because he mocked me. Said I was probably raised by wolves or something."

"And you *dated* him?"

"I was, like…nineteen," she says with a disgusted eye roll. "And he was kind of hot. Anyway, swimming is my weakness. I'm not a strong swimmer. We were out on a boat with friends one time, all talking about bucket-list trips. And while most of the others were talking about things like Paris and Tahiti, I said I wanted to hike through all of the national parks. Some of the others nodded or said that sounded cool. But the asshole that I thought was hot? He scoffed and said, '*Whatever. You won't do that. You won't even jump off this boat.*'"

"He sounds like a winner." I shake my head. I hate guys like that. "And what did you say?"

"I don't remember," she says. "I just remember being so pissed that he said I wouldn't do what I'd dreamed of. And I didn't give a shit about proving anything to anyone in regards to swimming."

"Yeah, you don't seem like the type to give in to peer pressure."

She snorts and sips more water. "No. I'm not."

"So, you don't like to swim, but you *do* like rafting?"

"As long as we're doing things right, I don't have to swim," she reminds me. "But if I have to, I can. I just don't like it."

"Gotcha. Are you close with your family?"

She narrows her eyes at me. "I think we've talked about me enough for one night. What about you?"

"What *about* me?" I feel my lips twitch as she lets out a laugh. God, she has a fan-fucking-tastic laugh. Throaty and sexy. I bet she makes all kinds of great noises. And that dimple in her cheek just begs for my attention.

"Tell me a little about you," she says.

"I'm from Montana. My family has a ranch outside of Cunningham Falls, and I live on the property. I also like to be outside. I love animals, and I work here in the park. That's about it."

That doesn't even begin to scratch the surface, but I'll be damned if I'm going to spend the night baring all of my secrets from my shitty early childhood to this woman.

"I grew up in LA," she says, surprising me.

"And you love the outdoors? City people are usually…indoorsy."

She grins. "Well, there are places to go near LA that are fun for *outdoorsy* things. I've liked to hike from the time I was small. But I'm dying to know what it's like to grow up in a tiny little town in the middle of all of these stunning mountains."

"I had the time of my life," I reply without thinking about it. "Fishing, hunting, running around. We skied, we played on quads, we chased wildlife off the property. Still do all those things, now that I think about it."

"You hunt?" Her violet eyes round, and she sounds appalled. "Like, innocent animals?"

"We hunt legally." I frown at her. "Do you really want to have this conversation? Because I can go into a ton of things like controlling animal populations and the need for families to eat, which will make your eyes glass over."

She wrinkles her nose. "Okay, I probably don't need the lecture. I just could never shoot at an animal."

"So, hunting isn't something we'll do together." I make a check mark in the air. "Check."

"The rest of it sounds fun, though," she says and leans back on her hands. "I've never spent a full winter in the snow. You know what the best thing about your house having wheels is?"

"You can avoid tornadoes?"

"That, and I can do pretty much whatever the hell I want. So, maybe I'll stick around for winter. It'll be interesting. And I haven't skied in forever."

"We have some of the best skiing in the world." I grin when she looks at me like, *really*? "I'm not exaggerating. People train for the Olympics here."

"It's something to think about," she muses while rubbing her hand through that gorgeous, thick hair. "Ugh, it's hot in here. Turn around."

I quirk up an eyebrow. "No."

"Don't be a jerk. Close your eyes."

I sigh but do as she asks. When I hear the mattress and blankets rustling, I crack one eye open in time to see Remi stand and shimmy out of her thick hiking pants, leaving her long legs bare. I see a flash of white panties before she sits again and covers her lap with the blanket.

"You looked."

"I'll apologize if it makes you feel better."

She smirks again and then smiles as she shakes her head. "I've been dying in those things. They're great for the trail, but not so much in front of a roaring fire."

She pulls one long leg out and plops it on top of the blanket, and I feel everything in me tighten.

"Now you're just taunting me."

"Serves you right for looking when I told you to close your eyes."

I take a sip of water and find myself reaching for her foot with a scowl. "You have blisters."

"Oh. Yeah, it happens sometimes."

I examine her heel where the blood has dried, and the hot red spot on the ball of her foot. Then, I dig my thumb into the arch and watch as her eyes practically roll into the back of her head as she lets out a long groan.

"If I pay you ten thousand dollars, will you do that until the end of time?"

Her feet are small, her legs lean and toned—I assume from years of being active.

And her skin is warm and smooth.

I move up to her ankle, slowly massaging around her ankle bone, and then smile when she whimpers.

"When was the last time you slowed down long enough for a little self-care, Remi?"

"Yesterday. I even took a nap and everything. Today was my reward for relaxing."

I'm not good at slowing down either.

I watch her face as I slide my hand up her leg, looking for any sign that she might not be comfortable.

Or might kick me in the face.

But she just bites her lip and lets out a little sigh as I massage her calf.

"Your calves are as big as mine, and I mean that as a compliment."

She smiles dreamily. "Thanks."

"Remi, if you want me to stop touching you, you

only have to say so."

"Did you bring me up to this chalet and arrange for a snowstorm so you could take advantage of me?"

I bark out a laugh. "I'm not that damn creative."

"The ten thousand dollars is still on the table," she replies and shifts so I have better access to her. God, she's just...*beautiful.* And when she finally lies on the mattress, flings her arms over her head in a stretch, and lets out a long, deep sigh, I know I'm a goner.

I want her.

I want every damn inch of her.

But I need to take my time. Besides, we're in no hurry. We have all night while the wind howls and the snow falls, as we simply wait in the safety of this place, in front of this fire.

With my eyes on her face, I lean in and press my lips to her knee. She doesn't jerk away or demand to know what the hell I think I'm doing.

No, she bites that plump lip again and, with it caught between her teeth, lifts her head and smiles down at me.

"You okay?"

"It's turning out to be a great day, thanks for asking."

I love her smart mouth. Her sass and sarcasm turn me on just as much as her firm, sexy body.

So, with my hands still roaming and kneading the muscles of her leg, my mouth wanders, pressing light kisses to her skin. And when she pulls that second leg

39

out from under the blanket and spreads herself before me, wearing just those little white panties and a black T-shirt, I feel like I've won the damn lottery.

"You're beautiful." My voice softly cuts through the silence around us, grabbing her attention. "You know that, right?"

"I'm okay," she says, her breath catching when I gently bite the inside of her thigh. "Oh, that's nice."

So, the woman likes some teeth. I can work with that.

As the fire roars nearby, I take my time exploring her legs. I kiss her calves, under her knees, and up the inside of those thighs until I'm mere inches from home plate.

And then I scoot up closer to her, clutching the hem of her tee in my hand, and push it up her stomach so I can uncover the skin there and continue my exploration.

Her fingers dive into my hair, and her breath comes faster. She's so damn responsive, so amazing. I want to strip out of my clothes and plunge so deep inside of her that I make us both see stars.

But I'm taking it slow.

She shoves the shirt over her head, and with her lavender-blue eyes hot on mine, she slips out of her bra and lies back once more, offering herself to me in the most stunning display I've ever seen in my damn life.

"If I wasn't already on my knees…" I have to swallow, unable to finish the thought before my mouth fuses to one perky nipple, and my hands take over, finished with the whole going-slow idea as Remi's hands pull on my clothes with impatience.

"Wanna see you," she says breathlessly. "You're just so tall and tanned and *hot.*"

I grin down at her. "You think I'm hot?"

"What do you think? I don't tear my clothes off for just anyone."

With a satisfied smile, I help her with my shirt, but before she can make a beeline for my pants, I cover her once more and kiss her long and slow, sinking into her softness. She's sweet and so damn potent, I have to pull back to catch my breath.

"Christ, I'm about to take you here on the floor, and I haven't even kissed you properly."

She licks her lips. "You can do that again."

"Gladly."

We become a frenzy of lips and hands, and she manages to get my pants undone, sliding her hand down into my underwear, wrapping a magical hand around my dick, and holding firmly.

"Well, helllllllo," she says in satisfaction.

"He says hi back." I nibble her lips, worry her nipple between my thumb and forefinger, and when her hand starts to move faster, I pull back and spread her legs wide.

If I let her keep jacking me off, I'll make a damn fool of myself.

Instead, I tug her panties to the side and lean in to

41

tease. To taste. To make her fucking crazy.

"Seth!" Her legs start shaking as an orgasm moves through her, and I grin against her, pleased as hell to watch her fall apart. "Holy crap."

"Again." This time, I sit up, plunge two fingers inside of her, and press my thumb against her hard clit. "Come again for me, Remi."

She shakes her head, but she can't control it. Her pussy pulses around my fingers as she flies even higher than before.

"Holy crap," she says again, completely out of breath. "Your turn."

Before I can reply, she attacks my pants, yanks them down my hips, and when my dick springs free, she wraps that sweet mouth around the head. With those magical lips, she proceeds to give me the best damn blowjob of my life.

She has the right touch, the right...*everything.* But before she can make me come, I push her back again because I want to see her face when I slide inside of her. I press her hands against the mattress and align myself with her hot, wet pussy—and then I freeze.

"Oh, fuck."

"What?"

"Fuck, fuck, fuck."

"What is it?"

I grit my teeth and close my eyes. "I don't have a damn condom."

I open my eyes and look down at her, finding a

disappointed Remi.

"Oh. Yeah, that's probably smart."

I kiss her lips. Her neck. I nibble down to her breasts.

"I thought you said no condom?"

"Doesn't mean we can't do a whole host of other fun things."

"But I came twice, and you—"

"I'm fine." I push back up her body and kiss her lips, more gently this time. "Honest. I'm not a jerk or a kid. I can handle it."

"On your back."

I raise a brow. "Huh?"

"Get on your back, Seth."

Who am I to argue?

I roll onto my back, and Remi gets to work, mimicking what I just did to her. She rubs me, kisses me, and when she makes her way down to my very hard cock, she settles in to drive me out of my fucking mind.

Lips and hands and then just a bit of teeth have me writhing and groaning until I come so hard, I'm pretty sure I lost consciousness.

But when I open my eyes, Remi's smiling down at me.

"Hi," she says.

"Hello. Am I dead?"

She snickers. "I don't think so." She pinches me.

"Ow!"

"Not dead."

"Wow, I'm so glad I arranged for this snowstorm."

She laughs and pulls her tee over her head. "Me, too."

I right myself, leaving my pants unzipped, then get up to walk to a window that I managed to uncover earlier. It's dark, the wind continues to howl, and it's snowing so hard, it looks like we should have a Christmas tree in here.

When I turn back to look at Remi, she's curled up on the mattress, her dark hair fanned behind her, and she's sleeping.

MY BACK ACHES as I roll over. Damn, did I fall off a horse again?

I crack my eyes open, and the events of yesterday flood back in: hiking up to find Remi and our night in the chalet.

When I look around, I see that Remi is gone.

I sit up and rub my hands over my eyes, then stand, throw on my shirt and shoes, and go off in search of the gorgeous brunette that I'm suddenly completely addicted to.

I don't have to go far. I find her standing in the kitchen with a steaming mug of tea.

"I figured out the gas stove," she says. "I lit it without blowing us up. Used some bottled water I found in the pantry."

"I appreciate you not blowing us up." I lean into her, the mug trapped between us, and help myself to her lips. They taste sweet. "You put sugar in your tea?"

"Just a little. I found a sugar packet in the pantry. It's handy that they haven't cleared it out yet this year."

"Is there any hot water left?"

"Plenty," she confirms. "Help yourself. I'm gonna step outside."

She kisses my shoulder as she passes, and when she's no longer in my view, I lean against the counter and take a deep breath.

I don't think there's been a time in my twenty-seven years that a woman has had such an impact on me. Emotionally *or* physically.

While my tea steeps, I nose around in the office and find a radio that I can use to talk to the ranger station.

I turn it on, and after several seconds, I'm talking to Roger, my boss.

"I'm glad to hear you're okay," he says. "What are the conditions? Over."

"I haven't been outside yet, but the wind is gone. I'll go scout it out in just a few, over."

"Let me know what you find out. If you need us to come up and help you down, we can do that. Over."

"Thanks. I'll be in touch. Out."

I walk back to the kitchen, grab my tea, and open the back door.

And when I step outside, I stop dead in my tracks and stare in horror.

45

"*I*t's okay," I assure Seth calmly as we stare at the big grizzly sow currently standing about twenty feet away. "She and I have been talking. She's not aggressive."

"I want you inside, now."

"Oh, I'm working on it, but I don't want to startle her."

"Look at me."

I can't. I can't look away from her.

"Remi, damn it, look at me." His voice is still low but firm. I risk a quick glance over, relieved to see that the door isn't as far away as I thought it was when I first panicked and saw the bear. "Ease this way. I've got you."

I swallow and smile at the bear. "Easy, girl. We're not going to hurt you. We're just going back inside, okay?"

I walk slowly to my right, and when Seth clasps my hand in his, my heart dislodges from my throat. When he pulls me inside and shuts the door, I let out a whoosh of air.

"That was an experience I don't plan to have again."

"You did so great." He tugs me into his strong arms and hugs me close. "She could have turned aggressive. They're eating and getting ready for hibernation. I should have thought of it."

"I'm okay." I pat his back and rub a soothing circle. "We're okay. But we'll have to hike down, and she's around. Maybe we can just live here through the winter. Or until she goes into hibernation."

His chest rumbles against my cheek as he laughs. "As fun as that sounds, I think we'll be heading down later today. However, there's a pretty big snowdrift covering the trail."

"I saw that, too. Before Yogi's wife came wandering over."

"The trek is going to be treacherous for a few miles. I don't know how far, to be honest. I'll call down and get a plan going with my boss."

"You have cell coverage up here?"

"No." He kisses my forehead. "I found a CB radio and called down to the station to check in while you were outside talking to Mrs. Yogi."

"Okay. I like that you can talk to other people and that we're not just left to our own devices."

"We would be fine even if we were," he assures me.

47

"Go enjoy your tea by the fire. I'll figure out what the hell's going on."

"I don't usually leave things in the hands of a man," I admit as I walk away. "But in this particular situation, I'm fine with it. You get us handled, and I'll be lazy. Until it's time to hike down. Does this mean I can't hike up to the glacier?"

I glance back and see his head whip up to stare at me in horror.

"You absolutely can *not* hike to Sperry Glacier. No."

"Killjoy," I mutter and sip my tea as I walk back to the fire.

The truth is, I'm tired. I don't know if it was yesterday's hike, and the ensuing adrenaline rush of running out of the storm that wore me out, or the energetic sexy times with Seth.

"Probably both," I mutter into my mug.

The man may be tall and well-muscled, but he can *move.* And he's strong. He just shifts me around like I'm a ragdoll.

It's not unpleasant at all.

I could get used to being touched, kissed, and coaxed to orgasm like it's his damn job.

"You're really deep in thought."

Seth sits next to me, resting his elbows on his knees.

"Just waking up."

"I figure coming face-to-face with a grizzly will do that."

I chuckle and then shiver at the memory of seeing that huge animal come walking around the building.

"I'm lucky I didn't pee my pants," I reply. "What did you figure out?"

"My boss is going to send a few guys up to help us down since we don't know where the snow starts. Or how deep it is in places. They'll have shovels. Probably take them a couple of hours to get here."

"But the bear—" I stop when he grins down at me. "What?"

"You don't have to worry. We're all trained to handle bears."

"Right." I finish my tea and set the mug aside. "We need to clean up our mess in here and put stuff away."

"We will. The linens will go in the plastic, and we'll put them in the laundry. I'll haul the mattress back up."

I nod, and we get to work, righting everything. When we're done, we sit on the two chairs by the fire.

"Do you have plans for tonight?" he asks, surprising me.

"I plan to burn these clothes and find a hotel to take a long, hot shower."

He raises a brow. "No shower in your van?"

"It's small and not always hot. I want hot."

"You don't need to find a hotel. You can use my shower out at the ranch."

I blink at him. "Is this your way of getting me to go home with you?"

The grin he flashes is quick and confident. "No. I'm offering you my shower. And a meal. That's all."

"That's all." I cross my legs and nod. "Okay. I'll take you up on the offer. Do you cook?"

"I was raised by two women who cook quite well," he replies. "They taught me everything I need to know. So, yes. I can cook."

"Do you have a favorite dish?"

"You'll find out tonight."

I grin, very much looking forward to seeing Seth's house and spending more time with him. And, most of all, a normal, hot shower. I wasn't lying. These clothes won't see another hiking day. I can't get out of them fast enough.

Even though our cells don't work well up here, we exchange phone numbers, and I take down his address in my notes. Just as we're finishing our plans, the door opens, and three men file in.

"You guys were fast," Seth says and stands to shake their hands. "How's the trail?"

"The first four miles up were fine," the tallest one says. "Then we hit snow. We're going to have a hell of a time for about a mile on the way down, then it lightens up."

"Thank you," I say as Seth and I load our packs onto our backs. "And I'm sorry for this."

"Just glad you're safe," another one says. "We'll be down in no time."

～

It took us just under two hours to make our way down. I was paranoid of bears, but having four strong men trained in what to do, helped me relax. They were also armed, so that helped.

My van started without a problem, and now I'm back at my campsite near Cunningham Falls.

Seth had some work to see to, so we agreed that I'd meet him at his place at around six this evening.

Which means I have a couple of hours to kill, and I'm hoping that Little Deli is still open so I can grab some baked goods for dessert tonight.

I quickly change clothes, grab my bike, and set off into town.

It's a comfortable sixty degrees today. You'd never know that the mountains are already dealing with winter-like weather. It's mind-boggling.

I can see that the deli is still open, so I park my bike and walk inside, noticing the nice woman behind the counter doing a little dance.

"Hi," she says with an embarrassed smile. "I'm so glad someone is here. Can you please, *please* stand here and keep an eye on things for five minutes while I run to the bathroom really quick?"

"Oh, of course," I assure her. "Go ahead."

"You're a lifesaver." She hurries off down the hall to the restroom, and I browse through the baked items in the glass case.

Someone rushes into the deli and then comes to a halt. "Where's Annie?"

I blink, realizing that Annie must be the woman who just went to the bathroom.

"She stepped away."

"I just need a cookie."

I eye the cookies, shrug, and walk behind the counter. Using tongs, I put the cookie in a little white sleeve and pass it over.

"That's two bucks."

He passes me the cash and walks back out, just as Annie returns.

"A guy just bought a cookie. He didn't want to wait," I inform her and hand her the money.

"Oh, that's Curt. He always comes at this time of the day for a cookie. Thank you."

"I'm Remi," I reply as I wander back to the customer side of the counter. "And you must be Annie."

"I am," she says with a relieved smile. "I have to tell you, after having four kids, my bladder isn't what it used to be. You saved my life."

"I only ever see *you* when I come in here," I reply. "No other employees?"

"My teenagers help me out in the summer, but now that they're back at school, I'm shorthanded in the afternoons." She narrows her eyes at me. "You wouldn't happen to want a job, would you?"

I laugh and shake my head, but then I pause. "Well, I really do like it in here."

"I guess so. You've been in almost every day for a week." Annie grins. "It's pretty simple, really. You'd just greet customers and fill orders from the case, and I'd handle making the sandwiches and soups and stuff. I'd only need you from eleven to three when we close. Wednesday through Friday."

"So just three days, four hours a day. That's not bad at all." I lean on the counter and smile at Annie. "You know what? I'll give it a go."

"Well, you just made my day," Annie says with a bright smile. "Why don't you come in tomorrow, and we'll fill out some paperwork and chat. Then you can start on Wednesday."

"That sounds great to me."

"Okay. Now, what brought you in to begin with?"

"I came in for dessert for later. I'm having dinner with a friend. I was thinking about that lemon meringue pie."

"Two slices, or the whole thing?"

"Oh, I think a whole pie is in order."

Annie laughs and gets to work boxing it up. "I think we're going to be friends, Remi."

"I think so, too."

ONCE I TURN off the highway, the road out to the Lazy K Ranch – as the sign said – is a little twisty, but not nearly as bumpy as I expected. I pass two other houses before I hang a right and find Seth's little house. It sits in some trees, with smoke coming out of a chimney, and his truck is parked in front of the two-car garage. I like his paint choice of simple white with black trim, and I immediately fall in love with the deep porch that spans the entire front of the house.

A girl could sit out there with coffee or a glass of wine and just listen to the nature around her all damn day. And probably into the night.

I park next to his truck, gather the bag I packed full of a change of clothes and my toiletries—along with the pink box full of pie—and climb the steps onto the gorgeous porch.

Before I can ring the bell, Seth opens the door, and a big black Labrador sits at his side, vibrating with excitement.

"Good boy," Seth says to the dog. "He's still a puppy and learning his manners."

Seth takes the box and lets me inside, and I immediately set my bag down and look up at Seth. "Can I pet him?"

"Go ahead."

I grin and kneel beside the big, happy dog. "Oh, you're a good boy, aren't you? So handsome and sweet. Yes, you are."

He licks my face and wiggles his whole body in happiness.

"What's his name?"

"Captain. Cap for short. He's only about a year old."

"Oh, you're just a baby. Yes, you are." I indulge in a few more puppy kisses and then stand, taking a deep breath. "It smells so good in here."

Seth smiles. "Shower or food first?"

"Shower. Definitely shower."

"Bathroom's this way." He leads me down the hallway to the master bedroom. "I have a guest bathroom, but this shower is better," he explains. "And if you only get an awesome shower every few weeks, you should take advantage."

His bedroom is a good size, with masculine linens and a big dog bed in the corner. The furniture is made of light wood, and the accents are in dark metal. It's quintessential farmhouse style, and I love it.

But the master bathroom is stunning.

"You have a soaking tub. A *copper* soaking tub."

The beautiful bathtub gleams invitingly in the light, and it makes me long for a lazy soak.

He nods. "Yeah, well. If you fall off a horse, sitting in a salt bath for a while helps with the aches and pains. You're welcome to use that, too, if you want."

"The shower is fine." But, man, I'll be dreaming of that deep, copper tub.

"Help yourself to anything you might need. I'll be in the kitchen making a salad."

He turns to walk away, but I stop him. "Seth."

He turns back with a raised brow. "Yeah?"

"I was going to kiss you first, you know, before the

dog. But I need a shower. Then you'll get all of my attention."

His mouth quirks up in a sexy smile, and he nods. "Fair enough. Take your time."

I take him at his word and move at a glacial pace. I've been traveling in the van for long enough that a real shower feels indulgent. It's a total treat. And while I don't mind the van at all, there are moments, like today, when I need the real deal.

So, I stand and let the hot water just pour over me. I wash my hair three times, and then while the conditioner sits, I shave my legs and wash my face and then stand under the hot spray some more.

This is just Heaven.

I briefly wonder if Seth would think I'm weird if I take another shower before leaving for the night, then shake my head at my ridiculousness.

When I finally emerge from the steamy bathroom, I'm wearing leggings and a T-shirt, my wet hair pulled back in a ponytail.

"If you'll show me where the laundry is, I'll put this towel in—"

I stop short at the scene before me in the kitchen.

A short, dark-haired woman has her arms wrapped around Seth's middle, and he's hugging her tightly.

"Uh, sorry."

The woman pulls back and smiles over at me.

"I didn't mean to interrupt anything. Obviously, you're busy. I'll just grab my stuff and go."

"Whoa," the woman says with a laugh. "I'm Seth's mama. I came over because he asked me to grab some garlic bread when I went to the store, and I forgot to drop it by earlier."

Embarrassment quickly replaces the anger and indignation, and I feel my cheeks flush when Seth laughs out loud.

But he quickly hurries over to me and kisses my cheek.

"Remi, I'd like you to meet my mom, Jillian King. She likely forgot to drop by earlier on purpose."

"Is it a crime to want to see the woman my son was trapped with last night?" she demands and crosses to me to shake my hand. Upon closer inspection, I see that she has a little gray threaded through her dark hair and a couple of lines around her eyes, but she does *not* look old enough to have a son Seth's age. "It's nice to meet you. I'm glad that you are safe and sound. Now, I'll see myself out."

"Uh, it's nice to meet you, too."

"Go report back to Dad," Seth says as his mom walks to the door. "And thanks for keeping Cap."

"Anytime. See you later." Jillian waves, and then the door is closed, and Seth turns to me.

"Did you really think that I'd be a big enough jerk to have another woman show up here while you're using my shower?"

"I mean, maybe she showed up unannounced. How was I supposed to know?"

"Mom's nosy. But, she brought the bread, and that's all that matters."

"Do I smell lasagna?"

"You do." He closes in on me and leans in to smell me. "Your shampoo smells damn good."

"Thanks."

"Before we eat, let's get something out of the way, okay?"

"Sure." I pucker up, but rather than kiss me, he keeps talking.

"I'm telling you, here and now, that I'm not seeing anyone else, Remi. I don't have any ties to anyone. And as long as we're seeing each other, that'll be the case. I'm not one to sleep around, and I'm way too busy to try to juggle women. Besides, only assholes do that crap."

"Agreed, on all counts."

He nods once and then leans in to press his lips to mine in a sweet kiss that's way too short for my liking.

The man can *kiss*. It's as if someone pulled him aside in high school and gave him an in-depth tutorial or something.

But then he pulls away and marches into the kitchen, where he uncovers a glass dish on the stove and pulls some bread out of the oven.

"I hope you're hungry."

"I am. Also, we have lemon meringue pie for dessert."

"I saw that. Little Deli is one of my favorites."

"Me, too. And I know I'm new to town, but I love it. Speaking of Little Deli, I'm working there now. I start next week."

His head whips up, and he stares at me in surprise. "You got a *job*?"

"Yeah." I tell him how it happened and then shrug. "I really like it there. And I like Annie, so I thought…what the hell?"

"Annie's great," Seth agrees. "Her mom started the deli about forty years ago. When Mrs. Blakely decided to retire, Annie took over."

"It's not a ton of hours, so I'll still have plenty of time for exploring. I don't know, I hadn't really thought about staying long term, but I like the idea of winter in Montana."

"I like the idea of you being here in the winter," Seth agrees with a grin.

"Yeah?"

"Oh, yeah. But what about the holidays? Will you go spend those with your family?"

"No." I take the offered plate, and we walk to the small kitchen table. Cap sits nearby, watching us closely in case we drop a morsel of food. "No, I don't go see anyone for the holidays."

"And you probably don't want to talk about it."

I grin and take a bite of garlic bread. "I'd rather not."

CHAPTER 5

~SETH~

*S*he looks so sweet sitting all curled up at the end of my couch, satisfied after her shower and devouring two helpings of lasagna, half a loaf of bread, and a piece of pie.

I love a woman who isn't afraid to eat, and watching Remi's lips as she chews is my new favorite pastime. When that dimple winks at me, it's a hell of a bonus.

"Oh, God, I shouldn't have had that last piece of bread," she moans and leans her head against the back of the sofa. "But damn, it was good."

"I'm glad you enjoyed it."

And I enjoyed watching her enjoy it.

"So, you said two women raised you," she says and leans her cheek on her hand, watching me with sleepy eyes. "I assume Jillian is one of them."

"Of course." I grin at her. "And Aunt Cara lives here on

the property with Uncle Josh. Two different houses, but less than a mile apart. I bounced back and forth between the two all the time as a kid. If I didn't want what one was having for dinner, I ran down to the other house. I'm sure it drove them both crazy, but it was a nice perk. Actually, my grandparents have always been close by, as well, so my grandma played a big part in my growing up also."

"That's awesome," she says with a sigh. "That you have so much family. And that you're so close to them. So, this is an old-timey homestead, then?"

I nod in agreement. "Absolutely. I'm the fifth generation of Kings to live here, and I plan to stay on the ranch until I die."

"And then your kids will, too?"

I shrug. "Nah, I'm not planning on having kids. But I have two brothers and a sister, and a couple of cousins, so the tradition will live on, I'm sure. We're a big, noisy family. The twins—my brother Miles and sister Sarah—are in high school. Troy's the youngest. He's in eighth grade and has more passion for this ranch than the rest of us put together. He'll help run it one day, I'm sure."

"That's quite an age gap between you and your siblings."

I nod. "What about you? Any brothers or sisters?"

"A few half-siblings," she says. "I have a really weird family dynamic."

"We all do."

She snorts. "Right. You have the all-American family out here on the perfect ranch in Montana."

I watch her for a moment and decide just to come clean. It's not like my childhood is a secret. I just hate talking about it.

"Jillian isn't my biological mother," I begin. "My dad married his high school sweetheart because she got pregnant—with me. He went into the military to support us. And while he was deployed, she fucked around on him. She was a shitty-ass mother, and one blessed day, she brought me here and dumped me off because she couldn't be bothered anymore."

Remi's mouth drops open, but I keep talking.

"I was a pissed-off kid. I'd seen shit I shouldn't have seen. And I had a chip on my shoulder. But we worked it out. I learned that my family loved me and wouldn't send me away. And Dad married Jillian. They had babies. They're my family. But believe me when I say that we're not perfect. We have moments that make me shake my head and question my paternity."

Remi's eyes bulge, and I laugh.

"Not really. I look just like him. What I'm saying is, no one is perfect."

"I guess I have a similar background," she says slowly. "My parents divorced when I was about eight. My biological father pretty much left without looking back. Mom remarried. Dale's not a bad guy, as in he's never been mean to me. But once they started having kids of their own, it was pretty clear that I was the odd kid out. I'm not close to them, and they pretty much just do their own thing. Sometimes, they invite me to things as an afterthought. Last year, Mom called me *on* Christmas Eve to ask if I wanted to come for dinner."

"Yikes." I hate that for her. No one should live through life without family.

"Yeah, well, it's not even hurtful anymore. I just don't feel bonded to them in any way. I don't wish them harm. They're just…strangers."

"So, you'll stay here through the holidays and make new traditions for yourself."

"Yeah." She smiles, her eyes still sleepy. "I like it that way, to be honest. It's easier, that's for sure."

She yawns, and I move over next to her.

"You can sleep in the guest room tonight if you want."

"I have the van."

"And I'm sure it's fine, but you're here, and you're tired, and I have an extra bed that's just sitting back there, not being used. You're welcome to it."

She sighs. "Okay. The thought of driving back to town and hooking up at the campground isn't appealing. I'll take the guest room."

I grin and lean over to brush my lips over hers. I'm gentle at first and then sink into her. She shifts so I can settle against her. As my mouth explores hers, she runs those sweet fingers through my hair.

Rather than deepen the kiss and strip her out of her clothes, I pull her to me and offer her a hug.

"I'll help you get settled."

"Thanks. I'll run out and grab a few things from the van."

She stands, shoves her feet into her shoes, and hurries outside.

I walk back to the guest room and make sure everything is in order.

When I hear the front door open, I walk out to greet Remi and smile when I see her carrying her pillow and a few odds and ends in her arms.

"The sheets are clean," I assure her as she follows me down the hall. "I had a college buddy stay a few weeks ago and washed everything after he left, so you don't have to worry about that."

"I'm so tired, I could sleep in the bathtub."

"Do you sleep in bathtubs often?"

"I did once, in college." She tosses the pillow onto the bed, sets her things on a chair, and turns to me. "It wasn't a nice big copper one, though. Can I be honest?"

"Always."

"I thought for sure you'd try to get in my pants, especially after last night up at the chalet."

I reach out and brush my thumb over the apple of her cheek. "You're staying through the winter, Remi. I don't have to rush it or hurry. I like the idea of taking my time, getting to know you. Unless you're so hot for me, you can't stand it and need me to scratch an itch for you."

She smirks, then looks me up and down in a way that makes me want to lick her all over. "You wish."

"Oh, so you're not as attracted to me as I am to you?"

"I didn't say that." She crosses her arms over her chest. "I can hold out. Probably longer than you can."

I bite my lip and watch her, enthralled by her. "You think so?"

"Sure."

"Wanna put a wager on that?"

She narrows those gorgeous eyes at me. "What kind of wager?"

"If you beg first—"

"I never beg."

"—you have to take me out for ice cream."

She lifts an eyebrow. "That's it? That's all you want? Ice cream?"

I nod slowly.

"Fine. And if *you* beg?"

"What do you want?"

She swallows, glances down, then looks up as if she's *really* thinking it over. "You have to hike up to the glacier with me."

I blink at her. "Remi, it's closed for the season. As you found out, hiking up there isn't safe."

"In the spring," she clarifies. "When it's safe. I want to see that damn glacier, Seth."

Win or lose, I'll go with her. Without hesitation.

But she doesn't have to know that.

I nod grimly. "Okay. Yeah, okay, I can do that."

She holds out her hand for mine. "Deal."

I wrap my fingers around hers and shake, then pull her knuckles up to my lips. "Deal."

"Now you have to leave this room," she says primly and pulls her hand out of mine. "I don't know why I'm so damn tired, but I feel like I could sleep for a week."

"We had quite the adventure," I reply, already regretting the stupid bet. What was I thinking? I want nothing more than to climb into that bed with her. "It was a long hike, a shitty night's sleep in the chalet, you ran into a grizzly, and then we hiked down."

"*And* I got a job today."

"You've been busy." I smile at her. "Get some rest, Remi. If you need anything, let me know. Make yourself at home."

I close the door behind me, then walk out to the kitchen to clean up from dinner. She offered to do it after we ate, but I saw how heavy her eyes were, how worn out she was, and I insisted that she sit with me on the couch instead.

I don't mind the clean-up. I've done more than my share of dishes over the years, and it's the perfect time to unwind, think about the day, and go over what's on tap for tomorrow.

It doesn't take long to load the dishwasher, hand-wash a few things, and wipe down the counter. I leave a light on over the stove in case Remi wakes up and wants something from the kitchen.

To be honest, I'm exhausted myself. I was scared out of my mind yesterday before finding Remi on that trail. My heart was in my throat as I rushed up the mountainside, worried that the storm had already killed her or that she'd gotten lost. So, now that the adventure is over and the adrenaline is gone, I'm ready to crash, too.

I don't have to go up to work tomorrow. Instead, I promised my dad and Uncle Josh that I'd help out in the barn, maybe ride the fence and make some repairs before winter sets in.

But they know that Remi's here, so I don't have to be at the barn at the butt crack of dawn. They'll razz me, but they would anyway, no matter what. It's just what we do.

But before I have fun on the ranch, I'll have some fun with Remi in the morning.

I've never been able to sleep late. It stems from years and years of living on the ranch, waking up early to feed animals and get chores done before school. If the sun is up before me, I'm either sick or stuck with a gorgeous woman in a national park.

The latter has only ever happened once.

This morning, I decided to make my mom's baked oatmeal and some bacon for breakfast.

"Something smells good."

I pause at the rough sound of Remi's sleepy voice

and then turn to find her standing behind me, her dark hair disheveled, and her violet eyes heavy-lidded with sleep.

"I made breakfast," I reply, rather than boost her up onto my kitchen island and have *her* for breakfast.

Her stomach growls, making us both grin.

"After dinner last night, I would have sworn I'd never be hungry again," she says and peeks around my shoulder. "But my stomach just proved me wrong. What are we having?"

"Baked oatmeal and bacon. I don't have any fresh fruit to go with it."

"Are there raisins in the oatmeal?"

"Yes."

"There. Fruit." She grins. "Do I have to do sexual favors to get a mug of coffee?"

I laugh and turn away, fetching her a mug. "No, coffee's free around here."

"How long have you been up?" She pours a little milk into her coffee, gives it a stir, then leans against the counter and sips. She's just in that oversized T-shirt from last night. No pants. I can't take my eyes off her slim, muscular legs. "Hi, my eyes are up here."

I laugh again and shake my head. "Sorry. I have a sexy woman in my kitchen with the best legs I've ever seen. It's hard to concentrate."

"Hard enough to *beg*?"

My eyes find hers. They're full of humor, but there's lust there, too.

I lean into her and kiss her forehead. Breathe her in. "It hasn't even been twelve hours, sweetheart. I think I can hold out a while longer."

She snorts, but there's disappointment in her eyes, and that doesn't hurt my feelings in the least.

"I've been up since about five," I inform her, answering her question.

"Good God, that's early."

"That's ranch life," I reply and scoop up her breakfast, then pass it to her.

"Do you have to work today?"

"Not up at the park. I have the next five days off. Now that we're out of the heart of the season, I only work three days a week. But I'll be putting in more time at the ranch now. There are some things I need to do today. What about you? What's on tap for your day?"

She takes a bite of her bacon then licks her lips.

Damn it. She's killing me. If she keeps that up, I'll be begging by the end of the day.

"I'm going to get settled back in my spot with the van. I really like it there. I can leave the van parked and ride my bike where I need to go. Super convenient. And then I'll check out some local trails. Don't worry, nothing crazy. Oh, and I have to go see Annie about some paperwork."

I lean on the counter and eat my breakfast. Part of me wants to tell her to stay here rather than in the van. The other part of me is like, *whoa.*

"Thanks for all of the food and stuff," she says as she rinses her bowl in the sink. "I had a good time."

"Me, too."

Before she can walk away, I catch her wrist in my grasp and pull her against me so I can take her lips with mine in a long, lingering kiss.

"I want to see you later."

"I'll be around." She grins, then pulls away and starts off toward the guest room. "I'll be out of your hair in twenty."

"You're not in my hair," I call back. I want to hurry after her. So, instead, I load the dishwasher and pull my boots on.

I grab a jacket and stop by the closed guest room door.

"I'm headed out, Remi. Just lock up behind yourself."

"Will do," she calls back.

I can almost picture her in there, the naked body I've already seen exposed as she changes clothes. I roughly tug on the jacket and stomp away.

I live far enough from the barn now that I drive my truck over. Used to be I'd walk from either Dad's or Josh's house, but I chose a piece of property with a little more privacy. I could still walk, but it would take too much time.

When I head into the barn, I see Dad and Josh, along with our long-time ranch hand, Louie, gathered around one of the stalls.

"She's a looker," Louie says, chewing on a toothpick.

"New foal?" I ask, and three pairs of eyes turn to me.

"A little filly," Josh confirms. "Born about an hour ago."

"You'd have seen it if you weren't entertaining a guest at your place," Dad adds.

Yep, they're going to razz me.

"Jillian says she's pretty," Josh adds.

"You're a bunch of gossiping women," I reply and shake my head. "The woman was trapped in a storm. I made her dinner."

"Spent the night," Louie puts in mildly.

"Whose side are you on?"

The old man just laughs at me. Louie's one of my favorite people in the world. He was working here when I came to the ranch when I was eleven, and he seemed to be old then. I have no idea how old he really is, but I've decided he's living forever.

Just out of spite.

And that's good because I don't know what we would do without him.

"So, are you all going to rag on me all day, or are we gonna get some work done?" I ask.

"We've been working since before the sun came up," Dad reminds me. "Miles and Sarah were here, too, before school, to watch this baby be born."

"I'll see them this afternoon. They'll be back out

71

here to watch her." My siblings all love the animals. It's in our blood. "Where was Troy? Is he sick?"

"Stayed in town with a friend last night," Dad says. "He'll be mad that he missed it."

"There will be plenty more," Josh says.

"Where are your kids?" I ask him. "I haven't seen Kim and Mike in a while."

"Kim was here with the others," Josh replies. "Mike stayed at Grandma and Grandpa's house, keeping Gram company."

I nod and look down at the new foal, just getting her feet under her. We lost my grandpa last year, and none of us have fully recovered from the loss, the kids have taken turns staying with Gram, adamant that she shouldn't be alone.

I don't know if any of us will ever get over the loss of Gramps.

"I'll have all the kids come hang out with me at my place this weekend. We'll have some fun."

"They'll like that," Dad says. "Now, let's get the fence mended."

We all saddle our horses. Magic's been mine for as long as I can remember. She's the love of my life.

"Hey, baby girl," I croon to her as I saddle her up. "How's my girl?"

She sniffs my hand, hoping for an apple or some carrots.

"I know what you want." I pull some baby carrots out of my pocket and offer them to her.

Before long, we're out in the pastures, riding along the fence line to check for holes. We have several hundred head of cattle that we don't want getting loose.

Rounding up a herd from where they're *not* supposed to be isn't easy.

As we come over a hill and gaze down on the meadow below, we see several animals down and plenty of blood.

"Son of a bitch," I mutter as Dad and Josh break off into a run.

The wolves are back.

CHAPTER 6

~REMI~

"It's just paperwork, nothing to be nervous about," I mutter to myself as I ride through town on my way to Little Deli. I came to town and hooked up to my campsite again, got the van all settled and ready to go, and then grabbed my bike and took off. The leaves are changing here as fall settles in, and there's a bite to the air that wasn't there just a week ago.

It's fascinating. And so different from southern California.

I kind of love it.

But before long, I'll need a heavier coat if I'm going to continue riding my bike around town. And once it snows, I'll just have to drive the van. It'll be a pain in the ass to hook and unhook from the campsite every time, but there's really no other choice.

I'm not going to buy a car. That would be silly.

I set the bike against the wall outside the deli and then push inside. Annie glances up from behind the counter and sends me a welcome smile.

"Hi, Remi."

"Hey there. I hope this is a good time to stop by."

"It's a great time. We're through the morning rush, and things should be relatively quiet until lunch. There are just a couple of forms to fill out, and I need a copy of your driver's license."

"No problem."

The business side of things takes less than ten minutes. When Annie tucks what she needs into a folder and turns back to me, I sniff the air.

"Do I smell peanut butter cookies?"

"Bars," she says with a grin. "They just came out of the oven. Would you like one?"

"Heck yes, I'd love one." I follow her back into the kitchen. There's a big doorway and a window so she can always keep tabs on what's happening in the front of the restaurant.

"Do you do all of the baking yourself?"

"My mom helps me sometimes," Annie replies and cuts into the bars. "She likes the early morning work."

"Seth told me that she opened this place."

"Seth King?"

I nod and bite into the bar and then blink in surprise. It's not too sweet. It's the perfect balance of salty and sweet and doesn't make my teeth hurt.

I could eat the whole pan.

"Yeah," I say after I swallow. "He's a new friend of mine."

"And a nice guy," Annie replies. "Not to mention, pretty damn handsome, just like his daddy and uncle."

"There is that. Does he look like them?"

"Carbon copy," she confirms.

"The Kings must have an excellent gene pool."

Annie laughs and sets the cut bars on a long, thin metal tray and then walks out to the glass counter to slide them in for display.

"You're not wrong," she says. "Anyway, yes, Mama opened this place in the early eighties. I practically grew up here. I sat in here and watched her bake or helped her with the soups and breads. I hated going to school because that meant I couldn't be in here with her."

"It's in your blood."

She turns a surprised look my way and then nods slowly. "Yes, I suppose so. I hadn't thought of it that way before. Anyway, she comes in a few days a week to help me with the baking, or she gets the soups simmering for me."

"Does she miss working?"

"Oh, yes." Annie laughs and nods at a young woman who walks through the door and claims a table to set up her computer. "She'd still work every day if she could. But she's older now and had a health scare last year. My dad is pretty good about keeping her reined in and makes sure she doesn't overdo it. Hey there, Renee, what can I get you?"

"Just a cup of that corn chowder and an iced tea," Renee says with a smile.

I watch Annie get the order together and take Renee's money. The transaction is quick and friendly and looks pretty easy to me.

"There's really not much to it," Annie says after Renee returns to her table. "I just can't do it all by myself."

"Well, I'm happy to help," I reply. "I mean, just being in here and smelling all of the delicious things for half of a day isn't a hardship. My hips won't be happy because there's no way I can resist buying a meal before I leave, but that's okay. It's sweater weather. I can hide the extra ten pounds."

Annie laughs and pats me on the shoulder. "I do like you, Remi. What would you like to take with you today? It's on me."

I pat my stomach that's still full after Seth's amazing breakfast. But having something for later would be nice.

"You know, that corn chowder sounds great."

"Would you like some bread to go with it?"

"Absolutely. Let's live dangerously."

77

WHITETAIL MOUNTAIN IS a ski resort in the winter and a hub of activities like downhill biking, hiking, and zip-lining in the summer. Most of the activities are closed for the season, but on the weekends, they still run the chairlifts for anyone who wants to ride up and bike down. Or hike up and ride down.

This afternoon, I'm going for the hike-up-and-ride-down choice. It's quite an elevation gain, but I don't mind it a bit. The trees up here are turning faster than the ones in town, and the air is cooler. My pace is quick as I climb the trail that leads to the summit.

Halfway up, I stop for a drink of water and gaze down to the town and lake below.

It's just so...*pretty.* It looks sleepy and quiet down there. Like something from a Hallmark movie.

I smirk at myself and turn to keep climbing up. The trailhead said this hike is just under five miles, which is a good-sized hike for an afternoon.

An hour later, the building that houses a restaurant, pub, and viewing room comes into view. I can see the top of the chairlift and notice a few people hopping on for the ride down.

I take a few minutes to walk around and take in the mountains that seem to just wrap around and hug me. If I'm not mistaken, I can see into Glacier National Park, Canada, and as far south as Flathead Lake.

It's a bright bluebird day with the biggest sky I've ever seen, and it's all simply magical.

There's so much to explore. So much to see. A person could spend their entire life here and never see it all.

I wander inside to buy a candy bar for the ride down, then walk over to the chairlift.

"You're lucky," the young man says as I approach. "This is the last chair down for the day."

"Oh, geez. I didn't realize it was that late. What time do you stop running them?"

"Five-thirty," he says. "That way, everyone is down by six, and we all head home."

"Well, now I know. Thanks."

I hop on the chair. He lowers the bar in front of me, and I'm off.

The ride is just spectacular. I can watch the town, the lake, and get lost in my thoughts as I leisurely descend the face of the mountain.

When I reach the bottom and am helped off, I decide then and there that this will be a weekly activity for me for as long as they continue running the chairlift.

I *could* hike back down, but why would anyone do that if they can take that ride?

The drive down to town doesn't take long, and when I pull into my space at the campsite, I raise a brow when I see Seth sitting on a log, waiting for me.

I park next to him, climb down from the van, and offer him a smile.

79

He grins back, but there's something in his eyes that tells me that he had a rough day.

"Wanna talk about it?"

He sighs, stands, and tucks his hands into his pockets. "Not right now."

"Shit day?"

"Yeah."

I nod and then gesture for him to follow me. "I have soup from Little Deli in here. Why don't I heat it up and we can eat together?"

"What kind of soup?"

"Does it matter?" I raise a brow and look back at him.

"Yeah. If it's tomato, I can't eat it."

"Are you allergic to tomatoes?"

"No, I just hate tomato soup."

I laugh and pull a saucepan out of my cupboard, then set it on the two-burner stove I have.

"Well, it's not tomato. It's corn chowder."

"I'm in," he says and pulls the door closed behind him. "It's bigger in here than I expected it to be."

I follow his gaze, taking in my tiny kitchen and the bed in the back.

"It suits my needs okay."

"Except when you want a good shower."

I laugh, then shrug. "I've stopped off at gyms here and there to go in and use their shower. I just pay a daily fee. I belong to a national gym that's really cheap, but they don't have them up here in the northwest."

"Almost everything up here is locally owned." He sits on the edge of the bed. "Are you safe in here? I mean, have you had any issues with creepers?"

I instinctively start to deny it but then stop myself. "Actually, only a couple of times. Mostly, people mind their own business. I have safety features in the van, and I have learned some tricks here and there."

"Such as?"

"Well, at night, I pull the seatbelts through the door handle, then click them in place. If anyone tries to open the door, they can't."

"That's damn clever."

"There are lots of little things like that. I watched a lot of videos and read tons of blogs before I decided to go ahead and do this. I'm a woman traveling alone, and I know that there are risks associated with that. Someone once suggested I get a dog, but it's not fair to leave it in the van for hours on end while I hike through the national parks. Dogs aren't allowed on the trails."

"It's the safest thing," Seth replies with a nod. "Wildlife might be attracted to the dog, and it puts both of you in danger."

"Exactly. I'm not willing to do that. To either of us. So, it's just me."

"Do you get lonely?"

I shrug a shoulder and ladle up the soup, offering him a bowl. "It's been nice to have the quiet. My life was such a zoo for so long, with so many people around, the anonymity is welcome."

Seth narrows his eyes on me. "Why was it a zoo?"

"You don't watch a lot of TV, do you?"

"No, no time for that. Are you a movie star?"

I laugh and shake my head. "Definitely not. You know those shows where people have to compete in physically challenging things?"

"Like *Survivor*?"

I smile. I won season thirty-six.

"Yes, exactly. I've done quite a few of those. It's been my job for the last decade, actually."

"You're kidding. You can do that? Just hop from one to the next?"

"Sure. I had an agent who got me booked on them."

"No wonder you're in such good shape."

"Not as good as I used to be," I admit and take a bite of the soup. "But, that's okay. I'm not getting any younger. I mean, I'm not *old*, but it's harder and harder to keep up with the kids in their early twenties, you know?"

"Oh, yeah. I know."

"And there's a lot of politics and kissing ass that's done. Plus, I dated a producer for a while who is kind of a jerk. It just wasn't *fun* anymore. And what's the point of punishing your body and dealing with all the bullshit of TV and social media if you're not having fun?"

"I can't argue with you there."

"So, I retired. And the calm and peace that I've felt since is a surprise. And it's pretty awesome. Because of the family dynamics I had growing up, I was alone a lot. It doesn't bother me. So, no. I'm not lonely. I'm having a good time. Meeting cool people, seeing incredible things. And, I have a new job."

"You must have gone to see Annie today." He sets his bowl in the sink. He's close to me now, and I can feel the heat coming off him.

He's a potent man.

"I did," I confirm. "I like her a lot. I think it'll be a fun job."

"I'm glad." He leans in and kisses my temple.

"So, what brings you down to town?" I ask and climb up onto the bed to sit with my legs crossed. He follows suit, sitting next to me.

"I had a bad day, and I was thinking about you. So, I came to find you."

Okay, that might be the sweetest thing I've ever heard.

"Are you going to beg? Do I get my hiking trip in the spring?"

He laughs and tugs me against him, wrapping an arm around me, and just holds me close.

"No." He buries his lips in my hair. "This is all I need for now. Some conversation and a hug go a long way."

I hear the exhaustion in his voice. "What happened, Seth?"

He sighs, kisses me once more, and then pulls away just a bit when I shift so I can look up into his face.

"Wolves," he says at last. "They've been pests on the ranch this year. Today, we discovered a small herd of cows about three miles from the barn that they got to. Killed eight calves."

"Oh, no." I take his hand in mine and give his fingers a squeeze.

"It was a bloodbath in that field," he says softly. "The mama cows were standing over them, crying."

"Jesus." I shake my head. "That's awful."

"Yeah. Well, we got the fish and wildlife people out there, and then we hunted down a whole pack of wolves."

"You *killed* them?"

His eyes are sad as he nods. "Six of them. We tried relocating them in the past, but they just come back. And our livestock isn't the only herd in the area that's been targeted. They can be incredibly destructive."

"I had no idea. I thought they were on the endangered species list."

"Not anymore," Seth says with a sigh. "I don't like killing animals. I know we talked about hunting up at the chalet. I think that's different, though. We feed families with that meat and keep the animal population down. But what we had to do today? That's shitty."

"I'm sorry." I lean over and kiss his cheek, then climb into his lap and hug him. "I'm so sorry."

84

He loops those strong arms around me and holds on tightly.

"Thanks," he mutters against my shoulder. "Thanks for being here."

"There isn't anywhere else I'd rather be right now."

CHAPTER 7

~SETH~

I didn't realize that we'd fallen asleep on the cozy bed in Remi's van. One minute, we were just hugging and talking. And the next thing I knew, it was dark, and I could hear an owl outside hooting away.

I check the time, surprised to see that it's past midnight. We must have slept a good four hours.

Or, I did, at least.

"Go back to sleep," Remi murmurs next to me.

"I have to go home tonight," I whisper and kiss her forehead. "I have to be up early so I can help with the ranch."

She sits up and flips on a light, then blinks at me, her lavender eyes heavy with sleep. "Okay. I don't remember falling asleep."

I grin and brush my thumb over her cheek. "Me,

either. We were tired. I want to see you tomorrow. Take you out for dinner."

"Like, on a date?"

"Yes, a date." But then I remember that I have a bunch of kids coming to my place tomorrow and swear under my breath. "Wait. Tomorrow's no good."

"Saturday, then?" she asks without hesitation. She doesn't look jealous or even curious about what I'm doing tomorrow night, and that's a breath of fresh air.

The women I've dated lately want a play-by-play on my whereabouts. It's damn annoying.

"Yes, Saturday is great. Pick you up at six?"

"Sure." She grins and scoots to the edge of the bed. "I'll walk you out. I have to secure the doors."

I open the sliding door of the van and step down, then turn back, noticing I'm at eye level with Remi's boobs.

It's not at all a horrible place to be.

She bends down and takes my face in her hands, planting one hell of a kiss on me that makes my head spin.

"What was that for?"

"Just something to think about until Saturday," she says with a grin. "Drive safely home, okay?"

I nod but don't walk away.

"You're still here."

"I'm waiting for you to lock up."

She tips her head to the side, studying me in the moonlight. "You're a chivalrous guy, aren't you?"

"I have manners," I reply honestly. "If that's chivalry, then I guess so."

"I like it," she decides. "Have a good night."

She pulls the door shut, and I hear her rattling around, pulling the seatbelts through the doors, I assume. After a few moments, the van goes silent.

She's likely back in bed.

It's true that I have to be up early to help out at the ranch. I could have just gotten up early here and driven out at the butt crack of dawn, though.

But if I stayed, it would have been way too hard to keep my hands to myself. And I'll be damned if I'll lose the bet after only twenty-four hours.

Saturday is a different story. I might be willing to beg by then and fuck the bet.

The drive home is uneventful, given the time of night. When I get inside the house, I crash on the bed, clothes and all.

I need to take advantage of the next four hours of sleep.

"Why can't I live with you?" Troy, my youngest brother says as I open boxes of pizza and pull out paper plates. All three of my sibs, Josh's kids—Kim and Mike —and even Layla, Ty and Lauren's daughter, are here.

Ty and Lauren have been my parents' friends for as

long as I can remember, and Layla is the same age as the twins. She's practically another sister.

"Because you have a house to live in," I remind Troy as I dish up some pepperoni and slide it to him. "With Mom and Dad."

"They're no fun," Troy says and frowns down at his pizza, then shrugs and stuffs half of it into his mouth. "They won't even let me ride the snowmobiles by myself."

"It's September," I remind him blandly. "There's no snow to ride on yet."

"Well, even when there is, they won't let me. They said so. I'm almost thirteen. I know you were riding by yourself by then."

"Not alone," I reply. "I had to take someone with me."

"So dumb," he mutters.

I glance into the living room and see the five older teens in a deep discussion about something, if the look on Sarah's face is any clue.

"You need to just ask him," Layla says, trying to keep her voice hushed. "He'll tell you. Seth doesn't keep secrets."

"Ask me what?" I ask and walk in to join them. I set a box of pizza on the coffee table. "What's going on?"

"It's nothing," Sarah says quickly and gives Layla a dirty look.

"Doesn't look like nothing," I reply.

Miles won't look up at me. Even Mike is quiet, and he's *never* quiet.

"Okay, you're all creeping me out," I declare and look at each of them. "Someone tell me what's going on."

"You're not our brother," Miles says, and I can hear tears in his voice. They're shining in his eyes as he finally stares up at me.

"Given that I held you mere minutes after you were born and named Sarah myself, I can guarantee you that I am, in fact, your brother."

But a knot has set up residence in my stomach.

"Not by blood," Sarah says, and her lip quivers. "You're not our *real* brother."

Six pairs of eyes turn to me, wide and full of questions.

"Where are you getting this information?" I ask in confusion.

"I have to do a family tree for school," Sarah says. "And when I was doing it, I found out that you're not my brother."

"Okay, let's settle this right here. Right now. I *am* your real brother. Dad is my biological dad."

"But Mom isn't," Miles adds.

"She didn't give birth to me, no," I confirm. I want to deny it all and tell them that whatever source Sarah used is wrong. I don't want to tell them about the shitty mother who birthed me, or the horrible way I ended up living at the ranch.

But I don't lie to these guys. Not ever. I want to be a person they can trust and feel safe with, so lying about this isn't an option either.

I rub my hand down my face and sit on the edge of a couch cushion. I sigh, brace my elbows on my knees, and look them all in the eyes.

"Our mom, Jillian, didn't give birth to me," I begin slowly. I cringe when Sarah's eyes fill with tears. "Dad married a girl just after high school. Her name was Kensie. And she was pregnant with me."

I tell them as much as I can without going into the gory details of the abuse and neglect that I went through. They don't need to hear it, and I don't want to relive it.

"And, one day, she told me to pack my shit because she was going to bring me to Montana. She didn't want to be saddled with me anymore because she wanted to have a life with her boyfriend. And I was ecstatic to come here, where I felt safe and loved. And when Dad got home from the Army, we figured things out between us. And then he married Mom and had all of you guys. We're a family. I'm your brother."

"Why didn't anyone tell us before?" Miles asks. "This is kind of a big deal."

"It's not really something I think about often," I reply. "I haven't been in contact with Kensie since I was about twelve. Mom punched her in the face and told her to stay the hell away from me."

"Holy crap," Mike whispers with a proud smile. "Go Aunt Jilly."

"She died," Sarah announces, surprising me. "Kensie did. I did some searching."

I sit back and stare at my sister, not sure how I feel about the news.

"When?" I ask.

"About six years ago," she replies. "I didn't dig too deep, but there was an article about an investigation. Sounds like she was murdered. I'm sorry, Seth."

"You don't have anything to be sorry about."

"Your biological mother was *murdered*," she says with all of the drama of a seventeen-year-old girl. "Of course, you're upset."

I smile softly. "I don't know what I am. Not surprised, really. She lived a hard life, and I'm just thankful that I didn't end up tied to her. I'm here with you, where I belong. Jillian saved me, you guys. She showed me what being a good mother is all about, and she loves me as if she *did* give birth to me herself. In her mind, she doesn't see me any differently than she sees you, and that's not always the case."

I think of Remi, and the opposite experience she had, and my heart aches for her.

"So, that's why it was never brought up. Because we're a family, and we just all moved forward."

"Did that Kensie lady do bad things to you?" Troy asks. He's always been the most perceptive of the group.

"Sometimes," I reply, and he launches himself into my arms, holding me tightly. He tries so hard, every day, to act so grown up, but then there are moments, like right now, when he's still very much a kid. "I'm okay, bud."

"I want to hurt her back," Troy says against my shoulder. "She shouldn't have gotten away with it."

"She didn't," Layla says, always the philosopher. "She was murdered. Mama always says, '*What goes around comes around.*'"

"Karma," Mike agrees. "She got hers in the end."

"I think this party has taken a far more serious turn than anticipated," I say as Troy sits next to me, keeping his head on my shoulder. "Are we okay?"

"Yeah, but I want to ask Dad about it," Sarah says. "I know, you're going to call me stubborn. But I have questions."

"I don't think it's wrong to ask questions. He'll probably be uncomfortable at first, but he'll be honest."

"I'll lead with a question about my period or sex, and then he won't be nearly as uncomfortable." Sarah's smile is just a little evil, and it makes us all laugh. "I think it'll make Mom cry if I ask her."

"Mom always cries," Troy says with a smirk. "She's such a girl."

"She cries because her youngest child is so ugly," Miles says to his younger brother. And just like that, everything is right in the world again. The boys bicker,

93

the girls giggle, and I know that, in a little while, I'll be up with my laptop, doing some digging.

We eat pizza, play some video games, and then Sarah dims the lights as they put the original *Friday the 13th* on the TV.

Kim keeps a pillow in her grasp so she can cover her face when it gets too intense.

Troy does the same with a blanket.

They all make me smile.

While they're engrossed in the movie, I sit at the dining room table and open my computer, running a search for Kensie King.

It doesn't take long for the information to come up. She'd been arrested a few times, and with each mug shot, she progressively looked worse and worse. Drugs were the charges the majority of the time, but there *were* two charges for solicitation.

My mother was a whore.

I shake my head and open the article about her death.

Albuquerque, N.M. – A woman identified as Kensie King was found in a vehicle in the Third Street parking structure by a building employee Monday morning. Authorities listed the cause of death as a gunshot wound to the head. Based on evidence at the scene, suicide has been ruled out, and the case is under investigation.

I frown and open another article dated four months later.

Albuquerque, N.M. – The investigation continues

regarding the murder of a woman found dead in a vehicle in the Third Street parking structure this past spring. Authorities confirm they have arrested and charged Cole M. Linton with the murder of Kensie King. His trial begins next month.

I end up spiraling down a rabbit hole, searching through articles about Cole—he was such an asshole—and discover that he was found guilty one year to the day after he killed Kensie. He's currently serving a life sentence in New Mexico.

"Do we have popcorn?"

I blink and look up to see Kim's pretty blue eyes staring down at me.

"Huh?"

"Popcorn," she repeats. "We want some."

"Oh, yeah. We can pop some. Go back to your movie. I'll do it."

She pats my shoulder. "I've got it. I know where the stuff is."

I look around and realize that they've paused the movie for a bathroom and snack break.

Knowing all I need to know for now, I close the computer and help Kim make the popcorn, then settle in with the kids to watch the last part of the movie. This, right here, is what matters. I've known that since I was twelve.

I set my past aside and settle in to enjoy the rest of my night with these young people, who are growing up too fast. Before long, the oldest kids will be off to college, and it'll just be Troy and me.

I glance over at my youngest brother, just in time to see him steal a handful of popcorn out of Sarah's bowl.

He has his own, he just wants to harass her.

And I'm grateful that, at his age, he's been protected and loved. He's never seen the kind of shit that I did at his age.

He's a *kid*.

Just as it should be.

"Is everyone ready to start it back up?" Mike asks.

"Let's do it," Miles says and tosses a kernel of popcorn into the air, catching it in his teeth. "Let's see some dumb kids get hacked to death."

"Don't tell your parents I let you watch this," I warn them. "They'll skin me alive."

"What happens at Seth's, stays at Seth's," Layla says with a laugh. "It's like Vegas."

"Can we have strippers?" Miles asks with excitement.

"Hell, no." I ruffle his hair. "You may not."

Half of the kids are asleep by the time the movie ends. The other three yawn and stretch, then turn over and sleep where they are when I turn off the TV. I grab empty popcorn bowls, take them to the kitchen, then quietly walk back to my bedroom.

My phone's been on the charger all evening. When I check it, I smile when I see a text from Remi.

Remi: *I hope your day was better today.*

That's all. That's the text.

I sit on the edge of the bed and think about how to

reply. I wish she had been here tonight. I think she'd get a kick out of the kids.

Me: *It was much better. Tomorrow will be awesome because I have a date with you.*

I set the phone aside but it starts to ring.

"I thought you'd be asleep," I answer.

"You just caught me," Remi says with a sexy, sleepy voice. "Also, I could say the same for you."

"I'm hosting a sleepover with six teenagers," I inform her and fill her in on my guests.

"That's a lot of hormones in your house," she says with a laugh.

"Oh, yeah. But they're fun. How was your day?"

"Good," she says and then yawns. "I hiked a bit. Don't worry, it was nothing crazy."

"Who says I was worried?"

"I could hear your frown through the phone."

I grin. "You can tell me all about it during our date tomorrow."

"Okay. I hope you sleep well."

"You, too. Goodnight, Remi."

"'Night."

CHAPTER 8

~REMI~

I haven't worn makeup in months. I don't even remember the last time I put on a full face of it and wonder if I forgot how. I stare at myself in the little mirror above my tiny sink and narrow my eyes. Four months? Five?

Either way, it's been a while. But I'm doing it tonight. Because it's also been a long time since I last went on a date, and even though I'm usually the type of girl in jeans and a T-shirt, I can be a girly girl, too.

Sometimes.

When the mood strikes.

And it struck today.

My hair is half up in a little braid, off my face, hanging loose around my shoulders. I might still be wearing jeans, but they're not torn or even frayed anywhere. And I'm in a nice, crisp white button-down top with a pretty rust-colored scarf.

With the last few flicks of the mascara wand, I survey my handiwork and decide that it's not too shabby.

"Good job, Rem," I mutter and return the mascara to my little, sparsely populated makeup bag, stowing it under the bed where it belongs.

I glance at the time and nod in satisfaction.

Seth should be here in less than ten minutes.

My phone rings, startling me, and I'm surprised to see that it's my mom.

Worried that someone is hurt—or dead—I answer immediately.

"Hello?"

"Hi, honey. How are you?"

She sounds too calm for someone to be seriously hurt, so my shoulders drop in relief.

"I'm fine, thanks. I'm in Montana for a while."

"Oh, how nice. Are you still adventuring, then?"

"Always. How are you guys?"

"There's not much going on here. Lilith and Britney are doing well in school. Lots of cheerleading going on around here."

"I'm sure."

"Anyway, I just wanted to wish you a happy birthday."

I scowl, pull my phone away from my ear, and stare at it.

"It's not my birthday."

"Of course, it is."

"Mom, my birthday is October twenty-eighth. Today is September twenty-ninth."

There's a pause on the other end. "Oh. Then who—? Oh, yes. That's right, I always confuse your birthday with your grandfather's. I guess I'd better call him, then."

"How?" I ask without thinking.

"What's that?"

"How, exactly, do you confuse your own child's birthday with someone else's?"

"Remi, there's no need to be dramatic—"

"Right. Of course. *I'm* the dramatic one. As always. Have a good evening, Mom. You'd better call Grandpa. And don't bother calling me on my actual birthday—if you remember at all. We'll consider this your obligatory call."

I hang up and let out a gusty breath. I should know her by now. I *know* that she's just not good at things when it comes to me. She's on top of it for her husband, for her other kids, but when it comes to *me*, I'm just an afterthought. She probably goes to my sister's games to watch them cheer every single time.

I played basketball. She wrote a check for the fees and dismissed me. She didn't even come to watch when we went to state, and that was a big deal.

I close my eyes, shake my head, and make myself loosen my shoulders, blowing out a gusty breath.

"Don't let her ruin your evening. She's already forgotten the whole thing."

There's a knock, so I rub my lips together and then open the van's sliding door, feeling a grin spread clear across my face.

Seth is also in jeans and a long-sleeved shirt, the color of ripe cranberries. His dark hair is still damp from a shower, and his ridiculously handsome face is clean-shaven.

I want to get my hands on him.

I want to sink my teeth into him.

"You're stunning," he says at last and shyly holds out a small bouquet of sunflowers for me. "I didn't steal these, by the way."

"Good to know." I smile down at the happy blooms, then turn away to quickly put them in a pitcher of water. With my wallet and keys tucked inside a small handbag, I step outside with Seth and pull the van's door closed, then make sure it's locked. "You look great, too. We look like we could pose for a fall spread in a magazine."

He looks down at both of us and then snickers. "You definitely do. But I'm no fashion model."

He's wrong. He's gorgeous. Better-looking than half of the people in LA, trying to hit it big.

He opens the door of his truck for me, and I climb in. Soon, we're off into town.

"Do you have a curfew?" he asks as he pulls out onto the main highway that leads into Cunningham Falls.

I laugh, but when I glance his way, I see that he's being totally serious.

"No, no curfew."

"Good. You may not make it home tonight. Just thought I'd warn you."

I raise a brow, but he just keeps driving as if we're talking about something mundane like what kind of toppings we like on our pizza.

"Perhaps I should have packed a bag?"

"I have everything you'll need."

Before I can ask any questions, Seth parks his truck in front of Ed's Diner. "I haven't eaten here yet, but it's been on my list."

"I hope you're hungry and that you don't have a problem with greasy burgers and fries. Because this isn't a health food place," Seth says with a grin.

"I'm okay with all of that."

He nods, jumps out of the truck, and hurries around to open my door. He takes my hand, links his fingers with mine, and leads me inside.

"Hi, Shirley," he says to the waitress, who greets us. "Two of us tonight."

"Sure, hon. Take that booth over there." She points to the far side of the room. "I'll be right over to take your orders."

"Thanks," Seth says and leads me through the restaurant. It's an old-fashioned diner, the kind with a long, white counter that seats at least a dozen people on glossy, red-topped stools. I can see into the kitchen where an older man bustles about in a white apron, filling orders.

The white tables sit on a black-and-white-tiled floor, and the chairs have the same red seats as the stools. The booths match, as well.

"Is that an authentic jukebox?" I ask and point to the corner where a colorful jukebox is lit up with vinyl records hung on the wall above it.

"It still plays," Seth confirms.

"This place is something out of a movie." I pick up the menu that sits tucked behind the ketchup against the wall and immediately feel my mouth water. "And I might gain fifteen pounds tonight. I'm not sorry about it."

Seth laughs, and I notice that he doesn't bother to look at the menu. Before long, Shirley circles around and pulls a pad and pen out of her apron.

"What can I getcha?" she asks.

"My usual," Seth says and then looks over at me.

"I'm going to do the cheeseburger and fries. And let's be crazy and add a Coke."

Shirley nods, jots it down, then winks and hurries away to put in our orders.

"So, you must come in here a lot."

Seth nods and reaches over to take my hand. "My Aunt Cara brought me in here when I was a surly teenager, and Ed made me wash a whole bunch of dishes. She was teaching me a lesson that day."

I blink in surprise. "Did it work?"

"Oh, yeah. I still had my moments, but I curbed the attitude a bit after that. I was an angry little shit."

I smile and try to picture this big, strong man as a hurt little boy. "I think most of us were a challenge as preteens."

"True," he says. "Okay, tell me about your hikes. Where have you been going?"

We settle into a nice little rhythm of my talking about where I've gone and what I've seen.

"When do the bears go into hibernation?" I ask, just as Shirley sets our plates in front of us. "Holy shit, that's a cheeseburger."

Seth and Shirley laugh at me as I goggle at the monstrosity in front of me.

"There's only one patty in there, right?"

"One patty and all the fixins," Shirley confirms. "Can I bring you anything else?"

"Please don't," I reply, shaking my head. "This might kill me."

"But what a way to go." She winks and walks away, and I shake my head as Seth takes a huge bite out of his own burger. Instead of a tower of fries to match mine, there's a pile of crispy onion rings on his plate.

"Will you slap my hand if I steal an onion ring?"

"No, I'll trade you for some fries," he says, and we make the exchange. "November."

"Huh?"

"The bears are usually hibernating by the end of November," he says. "But grizzlies don't always sleep all winter. Sometimes, they get up and wander around a bit."

"That's terrifying."

He laughs and munches on his onion rings. "It can be a surprise, yes. It's not often that they don't sleep all winter, but they've been known to do that. Most bears stay in their dens until about March, when things start to thaw. Why do you ask?"

"I'm just wondering how long I have to carry the bear spray. It's added weight."

"You *always* have to carry it." All humor is gone from his face now. "It's a permanent accessory if you're in the outdoors here for any amount of time."

"Even in the heart of winter?"

He nods. "Yep. Because what if Yogi decides he'd like to take a mid-winter walk?"

"Great." I sip my Coke thoughtfully. "Do you get a lot of wildlife at the ranch? Besides wolves?"

"We get everything," he says with a smile. "I had moose in my yard this morning."

"That's cool."

"They're beautiful. And can be scary, too. Any wild animal with babies is dangerous."

"Right." I watch him for a moment. "You'd be good at giving educational courses in the park. Or even at schools."

He smirks, but I insist.

"Really. You're smart, easy on the eyes, and fun to listen to."

"Easy on the eyes, am I?"

I wrinkle my nose. "I mean, you're okay."

Hotter than hell. He's sexy as sin.

"Uh-huh." He glances around and then slips into the booth beside me and leans in to whisper in my ear. "You're the sexiest woman I've ever laid eyes on, and I can't wait to get you alone."

He nuzzles my earlobe, kisses my temple, and then returns to his own side of the booth.

It's suddenly so hot in here, I have to take another sip of my Coke. Seth just smiles happily from across the table like he has the best secret ever.

But I'm going to make him ask for the sex first because I'll be damned if I don't get him to hike with me to that damn glacier in the spring.

"Are you ready to go?" he asks.

"I'm finished."

He stands and offers his hand.

"Don't we have to pay?"

"They run me a tab," he replies as I stand next to him.

"It really is 1956 in here." I chuckle and follow Seth out of the diner and to his truck. Once we're settled inside, he pulls away, and I recognize the route to his house.

I'm not insulted at all. It doesn't make me feel weird that he bought me dinner and now assumes that I'll just go home with him.

Because I *want* to go home with him.

I got a taste of what sex with Seth will be like when we were up at that chalet, and damn it, I want all of it. Every inch of him. Every sigh and nibble and thrust.

I. Want. Him.

And after days of aching for him, I finally get him.

The artist on the radio croons softly in the background as he drives the miles away from Cunningham Falls, but the silence between us is comfortable. When he turns off the highway and onto the road leading to his house, I'm not nervous at all.

I'm excited.

I'm *ready*.

I have visions of him yanking me through the front door and pushing me against the wall just inside, his mouth and hands hot with need.

I can't wait.

But when Seth finally *does* lead me inside of the house, he doesn't attack me. He doesn't kiss me or urge me back to his bedroom.

He tosses his keys into a bowl and turns to me from about ten feet away.

"Stay there," he says sternly but winks at me before hurrying away.

"Did he just tell me to *stay* like I'm a dog?" I whisper as I glance around. The two times I've been here, including today, his house has been so *clean*. Is he a neat freak? Does he have a housekeeper? It's a mystery to me because I always think of a bachelor's place as being sparse and probably messy. Full of beer cans and flannel shirts all over the place. I don't know why flannel shirts are in this fictitious picture in my head, but they are.

But Seth's home is tidy. And beautiful, really, with gorgeous caramel-colored leather couches and nice artwork on the walls.

It's just...*nice.*

"I like your couches," I say as Seth walks back into the room.

"Thanks. I do, too. Now, come with me."

He takes my hand and leads me down the hallway, through his bedroom, and into the master bathroom, where candles are lit, and the tub is full of steamy water.

"Alexa, play the first date with Remi playlist."

"Playing first date with Remi playlist."

Adele begins to croon softly through the speakers, and I turn to Seth in awe.

"You said that you liked the tub. You should soak and relax for a while."

I blink at him. "You want me to take a bath."

"Well, sure. If you want to, that is. If it's a stupid idea, I can drain the tub—"

"No, don't drain it." I put my hand on his arm and then boost myself up on my tiptoes so I can kiss him lightly. "I'm just surprised, that's all. I thought you were bringing me out here to seduce me."

His lips curve up into a little smile. "Maybe later. You've been hiking a lot, and I thought you could use a soak."

"It looks and smells like Heaven," I admit. "Okay, get out so I can get naked and sit in there. Do you want to join me?"

He frames my face in his hands and leans in to kiss me again, deeper this time. More intense than before.

"Next time," he whispers, then turns and walks out.

Good God Almighty, he does things to my libido that could be illegal in Montana.

Or any state, actually.

I strip down and set my clothes on a bench, then sit in the gorgeous copper bathtub that's been on my mind since the first time I saw it.

It's luxurious. It makes me feel...*spoiled.*

I've just leaned back and closed my eyes when there's a knock on the door, and Seth pokes his head in.

"Wine," he says and sets the glass on the table next to the tub. "And a little something sweet."

Chocolate.

Seth King just brought me wine and chocolate. In the bathtub.

And then, after a quick kiss and a lingering look at my body in the water, he walks back out again and closes the door behind him. Good God, that look could melt the ice caps.

"Did I stumble upon the perfect man in Montana?" I wonder softly as I sip my wine and listen to the music he curated just for me.

I just might have.

And the biggest question of all is: When spring

comes, am I going to be able to leave him behind? Will I want to? Starting a relationship wasn't on my radar. Especially not since the idiot in LA.

Okay, there might have been a few idiots.

Not that Seth has given me any indication that he *wants* a relationship. We're dating. Seeing each other. And, if my suspicions are correct, we'll likely be bedmates before the night is out.

That's not a relationship.

I lift my hand in and out of the water and watch the droplets break through the surface.

"Then what's your definition of a relationship?" I ask myself as Coldplay comes out of the speaker. "Because dates, sex, etcetera, are all indicators of a relationship."

And I'm wasting this gorgeous bath by overthinking the whole situation. I always overthink. I need to simply enjoy, take a deep breath, and deal with the rest as it comes.

CHAPTER 9

~SETH~

I only have an hour, tops, to get everything set up just the way I want it. That's if Remi lets herself relax with her wine. Soak in the hot water.

Just *be*. Which I don't think she does often. Though if I spend too much time thinking about her in that water, I'll throw my plans out the back door and go climb in with her.

I've never had the urge to spoil a woman the way I do Remi. And I come from a family of men who pamper their girls. Treating a woman like she's a queen, with the utmost respect, has been drilled into me since I was twelve.

So, it's coming naturally to me. I guess I just never had a person in my life before Remi that I *wanted* to invest in like this. I've dated nice girls, enjoyed the hell out of them, and treated them with kindness and integrity.

But I didn't want to move Heaven and Earth to see them smile.

Because Remi's smile can knock me on my ass from twenty paces, and I'd do anything in my power to keep that smile on her gorgeous face.

I have the fire lit in the fireplace. It's not nearly as big as the one up at the chalet, but it's all I have to work with.

I've just finished dragging all the cushions and pillows onto the floor. I could get a mattress, but this will be fine.

Besides, I have plans for the mattress later that don't include the floor.

I've barely set the bottle of wine on the floor with some more chocolate when I hear footsteps behind me.

I look back and just about swallow my tongue.

Remi's in one of my T-shirts. The hem skims her thighs, and her long legs glow in the firelight.

"My God, you're beautiful."

A smile tugs at her plump lips as I stand and take her hand in mine, lifting it to my lips.

"How was your bath?"

"I almost fell asleep." She leans in close but doesn't kiss me. She skims her nose over my cheek and buries her face against my neck as I pull her in for a hug. "Did you recreate the chalet?"

"Sort of," I admit, pleased that she noticed. I kiss the ball of her shoulder and then turn to survey the scene. I turned the lights out, so the only illumination comes from the fire. The pillows and cushions look inviting to me. Maybe I went over the top. "We didn't have wine up there, but we'll pretend."

She sits on the cushions and stretches her legs out to soak up the warmth of the fire. "This might be the nicest thing anyone's ever done for me."

I sit next to her and take her hand in mine, linking our fingers. "Well, this is pretty simple, really."

"It's thoughtful." She turns her face to me and smiles softly. "You're a thoughtful guy, Seth King."

"I have my moments. Sometimes, I'm a jerk, and my mother would likely tell you that I'm a handful."

"Mothers are supposed to think you're a handful," she says with a laugh. "I think especially when it comes to boys."

"And she has three. But my sister can hold her own."

"With three brothers, she has to."

"You're not wrong."

We're quiet for a long moment as we watch the fire pop and crackle in the hearth.

Finally, I break the silence.

"So, we need to talk about this bet."

She slowly turns her head, and I feel her stare on my profile.

"Are you begging?" she whispers.

"No." I swallow and meet her gaze with mine. "No. Neither of us is going to beg. Because we don't have to."

She nods once and licks her lips. "That's fair."

"I was always going to take you up to that glacier, Rem."

Her eyes narrow. "And I planned to treat you to ice cream."

"See? There's no need for a bet." I kiss her hand and then let it go to rub my fingers up and down her back and over her spine. "I think you're incredible. And I know we don't know each other that well yet, but I'm mind-numbingly attracted to you."

She's quiet for a second and then lets out a long sigh. "You're sexy, Seth. You have to know that. With all of those muscles and the chiseled jawline, it's almost ridiculous. But it's more than that."

She whispers the last sentence. I wait for her to continue.

"It's like I recognized you. Like part of me thought: *Oh, there you are.* And that sounds so...cheesy."

"I like cheese."

She lets out a startled laugh. "I'm not usually the cheesy type. I don't like mushy greeting cards. I roll my eyes at all of that stuff."

She shrugs as if she doesn't know what else to say.

"Well, sometimes mushy stuff is fun," I remind her. "Like when it's just the two of us, and we're sitting by a fire and establishing that we're attracted to each other. *And* that we have some feelings for one another."

"You have feelings?" she asks.

"Have you not been paying attention?"

She grins again, and it makes my stomach clench.

114

"Okay, so we're all up in our feelings tonight." She swallows hard. "Now what?"

"Now, it's whatever you want it to be," I reply honestly and refill her wine glass. She takes a sip and stares into the fire.

"Tell me you have condoms," she says at last, making me chuckle.

"I won't be caught unaware again," I assure her.

"Do you want to know what the best part of being at the chalet was?" she asks and turns her head to me.

"Tell me."

"Your hands on me."

I feel the smile spread and know—without a doubt in my mind—that this is the invitation I've been looking for.

I take the wine out of her grasp and set it aside, then guide her down onto the cushions the way I did in the chalet just a week ago.

"The best part," I say and kiss the inside of her ankle, "was exploring you. Every single inch of you. And I intend to do the same tonight. I'm taking it slow with you."

"So, you're trying to kill me, then." She gasps when I lick the underside of her knee. "Death by torture."

"I want you to lie back, empty that busy brain of yours, and just enjoy yourself. Enjoy *us*." I kiss her calf as I press my thumb into the arch of her foot and make her moan deliciously.

And when I kiss the inside of her thigh, and she

arches her back, gripping a pillow like a lifeline, I can barely hold myself back from taking her right here and now.

But I'm taking it slow.

I let my fingertips linger on the elastic of her panties, and when I slide the fabric down her legs and open her wide, I'm met with a wet, gorgeous pussy.

Her fingers dive into my hair as I work her over with my mouth, licking and teasing the hard nub of her clit until her legs shake uncontrollably.

"I can't," she moans as she tries to catch her breath. "I can't do it again."

"You can." I push my hand under the hem of her shirt and cup her breast, brushing my thumb over the hard peak of her nipple. With my other hand, I press one finger inside of her. "Give me one more, Remi."

"Oh, shit." She arches her neck and succumbs to wave after wave of pleasure as it moves through her. When she settles a bit, she opens those vibrant, violet eyes and stares at me as I lick my finger clean. "You're way overdressed for this."

She sits up and reaches for my belt. Her movements are painfully slow, and I reach down to help, but she bats my hands away.

"No way, cowboy. It's my turn to tease the hell out of you."

"Fair's fair, I guess."

She grins up at me, unfastens my jeans, and then slides her hand inside, the back of her hand flat against

116

my stomach until her fingertips brush over my already hard and pulsing cock.

I might go cross-eyed.

And, frankly, I don't care.

I've never been so thoroughly worked over. As if it's someone's job in life. She's slow and steady, using both her hands and her mouth to drive me out of my mind with pleasure and desire for her.

"I will not come in your mouth," I growl as I take her shoulders in my hands and ease her away. "I feel like I've waited eons to be inside of you, damn it."

Her smile is full of female satisfaction as she threads her fingers through my hair once more and moves to straddle my lap.

"I think we should remedy that."

"Hold on."

I fumble through the throw blankets and find the foil packet I stashed there earlier, but before I can roll the condom on, she takes it from my grasp and does it for me.

She sheaths me her damn self.

"I'm keeping you forever," I say, making her laugh. When the condom is on all the way, Remi slowly lowers herself over me until she's seated fully, staring into my eyes. "Jesus you're snug."

She rests her forehead against mine. "I think you're big."

That makes me flash a smile. "Maybe both."

She starts to move her hips, back and forth,

grinding and clenching. I ball the hem of the T-shirt she's wearing and pull it over her head, tossing it onto the floor next to us.

"Your skin is pure sin in the firelight," I murmur.

"I was thinking the same about you," she whispers. "God, you do things to me."

"That's my line." I cup her ass and move her onto her back, brace myself over her, and take control of the rhythm. The strokes are long and deep. Slow.

I lower my lips to hers, sinking into her. Her long legs wrap around my waist, and it feels like coming home.

Like this, like *she* is where I'm supposed to be.

"So beautiful," I whisper and pick up the pace when she brazenly cups my ass and urges me to go faster. "So demanding."

She bites my shoulder. "You haven't seen anything yet."

We laugh. She sighs. I groan.

And, finally, here in front of the fire in my little house, we lose control and succumb to the fire burning inside of us.

"Holy," she says and swallows hard as she catches her breath, "shit."

"Yeah."

I fall onto my back and stare at the exposed wood beams of my ceiling.

"That's it?" she asks. "That's all you have to say?"

"Can't talk." I shake my head. "Dead."

Remi giggles and rolls over onto my chest, pinching my stomach.

"Ouch."

"You're not dead," she says and kisses my cheek. "Yet."

"If this isn't Heaven, I don't know what is."

"How do you do that?"

I find enough strength to glance down at her. "Do what?"

"Always say the nicest things. Do you have a script somewhere that you've memorized?"

"No." I chuckle and brush a few pieces of her hair behind her ear. "I just say what I think."

"Did you have special coaching for this?"

She yelps as I reverse our positions and hover over her once more. "I'm sorry that the assholes before me weren't nice to you. If they were, you wouldn't be taken off guard when I say things that are flirty or compli-mentary."

"I didn't…I haven't—"

"I suggest you get used to it." I kiss her softly. "Because I plan to have sex with you and say mushy things to you often. As often as possible."

"I mean, we have jobs," she reminds me. "And other responsibilities."

"And then I can be with you," I reply. "Now, I'm hungry again. Do you want some leftover pizza from last night? I can pop it in the oven."

119

She blinks at me and then nods. "Yeah. Yeah, I want pizza."

"Awesome."

I hop up, pull on my boxers, and pad into the kitchen where I turn on the light over the stove, preheat the oven, and pull out the box of leftovers from the fridge.

"What kind do you have?" she asks from behind me.

"Pepperoni and sausage. Or chicken and bacon with a white sauce."

"I want both."

I raise a brow and glance down at her. She's back in my T-shirt, and her dark hair screams: *I just had crazy-great sex*.

I want her all over again.

"Feed me before you fuck me," she warns me, narrowing her eyes.

"Strict," I mutter. "I'll heat it all up. I have some breadsticks, too."

"I'll take all the carbs. I worked up an appetite."

I slide everything onto the rack in the oven and prop my hands on my hips as I turn back to her. "What should we do while it heats up?"

She lifts a shoulder. "Wanna sit on your porch?"

"It's like forty-five degrees outside."

"We'll take a couple of these blankets. I *love* that porch, Seth. I need to sit on it."

"Okay." She can have whatever she wants.

I put some more clothes on and, armed with blankets, lead her outside to sit on the swing my dad helped me hang last summer.

"I've never seen so many stars," she says with a hushed voice. "You can't see them well in the city."

"It's a big sky," I agree. "In a couple of months, we'll have aurora borealis shows on display."

"I've never seen the northern lights," she says with a smile. "Oh, I can't wait."

"I'm going to go get the pizza. Are you okay out here alone?"

"Do I need bear spray?" Her voice is full of jest, but I nod soberly.

"You might. But, I doubt it."

"Just hurry," she suggests.

It doesn't take me long to return the pizza to the box and move to the porch where Remi's huddled under a blanket, staring dreamily at the stars.

"We're literally in the middle of nowhere," she says as I sit next to her, and she takes a slice of pizza. "It feels like we're the only humans for hundreds of miles."

"My parents are less than a mile that way." I point to the north. "And my aunt and uncle are a mile and a half that way." I point to the east.

"Don't burst my bubble."

I grin and take a bite of the pepperoni and sausage.

"You don't get lonely out here?"

"There's no time for that. I fall into bed at night, exhausted, and I'm back up before the sun to work. My family is close, and my friends are just in town. But I've lived out here on the ranch for more than fifteen years, Rem. It's all I know. All I care to know."

"You don't think you'll move away?"

"No. I'm a cowboy. I like my little spot in the world."

"It's a good spot." She finishes a slice and then reaches for another. "And I was right about this porch. It's the bee's knees."

I raise a brow at her. "The bee's knees?"

"Mm." She chews thoughtfully. "Yeah. It's pretty great. I'd be out here all the time."

"So, you're going to keep seeing me for my porch?"

"That and that sweet tongue of yours."

"Like what I can do with my tongue, do you?"

She shakes her head and nudges me with her shoulder. "Don't hog all the pizza."

CHAPTER 10

~REMI~

Someone is knocking on the door of my van.

I turn on a light and blink in confusion as I look around my vehicle. It's six o'clock in the damn morning.

Knock, knock.

"Yeah, yeah, I'm coming." The only downside to this van is, there's no peephole to look out and see who's at the door. "Who is it?"

"Seth."

I unlock and open the door, and cold air blows inside.

"Is something wrong? Is everyone okay? I don't know how I can help, but I will if I can. What's going on?"

He grins and steps up into the van. He has to duck just a smidge so he doesn't hit his head on the ceiling.

"Everyone's fine." He closes the door and sets a tray of coffees on my counter, then pulls me against him for a big hug. "But I kind of love it that you automatically switched into helper mode."

"I mean, people don't usually show up at my door this early unless something's wrong."

"I tried to call," he says.

"I don't have the sound on." My voice is muffled against his chest. "Are you okay?"

"Yeah." He kisses the top of my head. "I know you're starting your new job today, and I wanted to bring you some coffee. I have muffins, too. Mom made them early this morning."

I pull back to stare up into his soft brown eyes. "At six?"

"I think she was up around four."

"No, I mean, it's awfully early for you to come by."

"I have to work myself, and I've been up for a couple of hours already, taking care of a new foal we have in the barn." He grins and leans down to kiss me. If Seth ever decided to start charging for his kisses, he'd be independently wealthy within an hour.

"I have so many questions, but I'm not awake enough to ask them."

He chuckles and passes me a coffee. "I know it's early, but I'm not sorry. I wanted to see you this morning."

"You don't have to be sorry," I assure him and climb

back up onto the bed with my coffee. "You're always welcome here. This is good coffee."

"I have a busy day ahead, so I can't stop into Little Deli to see you later."

"It's okay, Seth."

"Well, I can celebrate with you tonight. Are you up for a double date?"

I cock a brow and take another sip of coffee. "With whom?"

"My best friend, Gage, and a girl that he's recently started dating. Her name is Tate. She's nice, you'll like her."

"Sure, that could be fun."

He smiles and leans over to kiss me once more. I set the cup aside and lay my hands on his face tenderly. He turns to press his lips to my palm.

"Thank you," I whisper. "For the coffee and for making me feel special today."

"You're welcome." He kisses me once more. "Now, I have to go before I tumble you back into that bed and call in sick to work."

I laugh and shake my head. "There's time for that later."

"You should have stayed last night."

I press my lips together. "I've been staying at your place since our first date, Seth. I can't just leave my van here, empty."

He looks like he wants to say more, but he just

shakes his head slowly, kisses me lightly, and turns to the door.

"Have a great first day. I'll pick you up at five."

"Thank you. You have a good day, too, cowboy."

He winks, and then he's gone. I hear his truck start and pull away, and I lie down to stare at the ceiling.

It would be so damn easy to fall in love with Seth King. What's not to love?

"You're enjoying a nice man while you're in Montana for the winter," I remind myself. "You're not here to fall in love. You're not staying. Try to remember that."

I reach over and snag the bag of muffins off the counter and moan when I realize they're still warm from the oven.

I bite into a banana muffin with chocolate chips. Dear God, do they eat like this every day? Whose mother bakes fresh muffins at four a.m.?

I take another bite, then a sip of coffee.

Apparently, the King family does.

Lord help me.

"How can I help you?"

I'm an hour into my first shift, and I officially love this job. Annie's the sweetest person ever, and the customers are fun.

"I'll have one of those turkey-stuffed croissants," the

customer says, looking in the case of goodies. "And a huckleberry scone."

"Those are my favorite," I confide with a wink.

"Annie and her mama have a way in the kitchen," he replies. "I'm Noah. I don't think I've seen you before."

"I'm Remi, and you probably haven't. I'm new in town."

"Well, welcome, Remi."

I pass him his bag of goodies. Once he pays, he nods and walks out.

"He looks familiar," I say to Annie after the door closes behind him.

"The King family resemblance is strong," she replies. "He's a cousin of Seth's."

"Are they related to the whole town?"

She laughs and slides a fresh tray of lemon bars into the case. "Not the *whole* town. But theirs *is* a big family. Speaking of, here's Seth's daddy and uncle now."

I turn as two men walk through the door. They're the spitting image of each other, and I can see where Seth gets his strong, handsome features.

"Good morning," I say with a smile. "What can I get for you?"

"I need a sandwich," the one on the right says. "Turkey with cheddar and extra onions."

"Dude, Cara won't let you kiss her."

Extra onions must be Josh.

"Cara lets me kiss her no matter what." Josh's smile

127

is cocky as he turns to me. "You must be Remi. Seth has told us all about you."

"So you came in to check me out?" I guess.

"Just to say hello," Zack replies easily and leans on the counter. "And I'll take a breakfast burrito and three peanut butter cookies."

I fill their orders and laugh at their antics. They give each other a hard time but laugh easily.

Yes, I can clearly see where Seth gets a lot of his personality as well as his looks.

"Have a great first day, Remi," Zack says before the two of them leave.

"Thanks. Enjoy your lunch." I turn when I hear Annie giggle. "What?"

"I think it's cute, that's all."

"What's cute?"

"The fact that Seth has clearly talked about you with his family and that they're coming in to say hello. It's nice. You're clearly more than friends."

"Is it weird?"

Her smile fades, and she tips her head to the side, staring at me. "Why would it be weird?"

"We just started seeing each other. Isn't it soon for him to tell his family about me?"

"I guess that depends on the person. Seth's close to his family, so it doesn't surprise me that he confided in them. If he's moving too fast for your comfort, you only need to say so, Remi. It's natural for him to be open with his family."

"And it's not natural for me," I reply softly. "Because I'm not close to mine the way he is. But that doesn't mean he's done anything wrong."

"Agreed." She pats my shoulder. "Okay, I have to check on the last of the soup I have on the stove. We're about to get busy for lunch, so I'll come out and help you."

"Thanks."

She's not wrong. We do get busy, with a line to the door at one point, which makes the time fly. Everyone smiles and introduces themselves to me.

The owner of the yoga studio, Fallon, who happens to be married to Noah, invites me to a class for free. Even the police chief, Brad Hull, stops in for his lunch.

"I'll never remember everyone's names," I mutter to Annie as I fill a bag with bagels for a nice woman named Aspen.

"You'll remember Aspen," she whispers. "She's married to Prince Callum."

I stare at her and almost swallow my tongue when I stand up and smile at the princess. "Here are your bagels. Um, Your Highness?"

Aspen's smile is kind. "Just Aspen around here. Thanks for the bagels, Annie. I ran out down at Sips."

"Just call if you need more, and I'll bring some down."

"You're the best," Aspen says as she hurries out. "Nice to meet you, Remi!"

When the door closes behind her, I turn to Annie, who's laughing into her hand.

"You could have warned me!"

"Aspen owns Drips & Sips, the café down the block. And, yes, she's a princess. The royal family all lives here part-time. They're casual about it and don't expect anyone to bow or curtsy."

"I don't even know *how* to curtsy," I mutter, then turn to smile at the three women who come through the door. "Good morning. Or, afternoon now, I suppose."

"Hi there," the brunette says, and then I realize that I know her already.

"Hi, Jillian."

Zack's wife.

I can hear Annie laughing in the kitchen. She must have run back there to hide her delight.

"This is Cara and Lauren. We thought it would be fun to stop by for a little snack."

"It's nice to meet you both. The muffins that Seth brought this morning were amazing," I tell Jillian. "Thank you so much."

"Oh, he did bring them by. I'm glad. And you're welcome."

"You're beautiful," Lauren says. "Jillian didn't exaggerate."

I feel my cheeks heat. "Thank you."

"It's probably a little over-the-top to come by," Cara adds. "But when Seth told us you'd be here today, we wanted to come say hello and wish you well."

"Thank you," I say again and soften a little. Annie sets some treats on the counter.

"Annie knows what we like," Jillian explains. "And don't worry, you'll learn. I hope you have a great day."

"You, too," I reply and turn to stare at Annie after the three women choose a table near the back to enjoy their snacks. "They literally *all* came in to check me out."

"Not all of them," Annie replies, but her eyes are dancing with humor. "It's sweet. They mean well."

"They're very nice," I concede.

The afternoon slows down a bit. Just before we close, a bunch of kids file through after school to buy up the rest of the baked goods.

When we finally lock the door, I turn to Annie and sigh. "How did you do this by yourself?"

"I've been doing it for a long time," she replies. "But I'm so glad you took the job. You're a natural. The customers like you, plus you're efficient and smart. Please don't quit."

"I don't plan to quit," I reply with a laugh. "I liked it. Also? It's good exercise."

"Hell, yes, it is. You're on your feet, reaching and pulling, bouncing around back and forth. It's hard work."

"It's a good thing I'm not afraid of hard work."

She grins again. "I like you a lot, Remi."

~

"How was your day?" Seth asks after I'm settled in his truck, and we're driving into town to meet his friends for dinner.

"Busy," I reply. "I like it there. The job is fun. It's a lot of work, but that's okay because I could use the exercise. Also, I think I met most of your family today."

His head whips over in surprise. "What?"

I tell him about his parents, his aunt and uncle, and Lauren coming to the deli today.

"Hell. I'm sorry, Remi. I mentioned that you were starting your job, but I didn't intend for them to all show up and give you the third degree."

His cheeks have reddened, and he looks...*embarrassed.*

"They didn't hurt anything. I was surprised. Annie thought it was hilarious. But it was funny more than anything."

He sighs, so I reach over to take his hand. "Honest, Seth. It's no biggie."

Seth just shakes his head and parks his truck in front of a little Italian restaurant called Ciao.

"I hope you like pasta," he says.

"Are there people who *don't* like pasta?" I ask, making him laugh before he exits his truck and walks around to open the door for me. "It's a cute place."

"And usually busy," he replies. "But we have reservations."

He escorts me inside, and we're shown to a table where Gage and who I assume is Tate are already seated. After the introductions, and once we're settled in with wine and our orders placed, Tate leans on the table and smiles over at me.

"I'm a reality show junkie," she says. "I've seen you on TV. Is all of that real, or is it staged?"

I grin and sip my wine. "Well, it's real. Trust me. When I dislocated my shoulder while climbing El Capitan on *Death Defy*, it felt very real. They don't dictate who wins. But they do make us wear certain clothes or wear makeup, and that's a pain in the ass, especially when you sweat so much."

"No kidding," Tate says. "I saw that fall in Yosemite. It looked horrible."

"Not my finest day," I agree. "What do you do, Tate?"

"I work in interior design."

"Oh, that's fun," I reply as I hear Gage and Seth talk about something going on in the park. "I bet you get to see some beautiful homes."

"I do. I've designed some amazing spaces. Are you renting while you're in town?"

"No, I have a travel van."

She blinks at me for a moment. "You live in your van?"

"Yep. I know it sounds weird, but it works for me."

"It's not weird, just surprising. You really are an

133

adventurer. I love it. Some of those travel vans are gorgeous."

"What do you do, Gage?" I ask when there's a lull in the conversation.

"I was in the Army for a while. Now, I do private training and rehab. That's how I met Tate."

"Really?" I look between the two and then at the cane resting against the table.

"I had a stroke," Tate says. "And because of it, I couldn't walk or do anything really. I had to relearn. And Gage has been the one to teach me. I've been out of the wheelchair for a couple of weeks."

"That's *amazing*." I shake my head and then lean back so the waitress can set my pasta in front of me. After she tops our dishes with fresh cheese and promises to return with more of the *delicious* garlic bread, I turn back to Tate. "You can't be thirty."

"Just over."

"And you had a stroke?"

She nods and carefully puts a bite of food in her mouth. "I did. But I'm doing much better now."

The four of us fall into an easy conversation, and before I know it, we're finishing dessert. Seth was right. I like his friends.

I like them a lot.

And I respect the hell out of them.

"We should do this again," I say as we walk out of the restaurant. Tate walks with the cane, but she's not slow. "I had a great time."

"I'm game," Gage says. "Welcome to Cunningham Falls, Remi. It was nice to see you again."

I watch as Gage puts his hand on the small of Tate's back and patiently walks with her to his SUV. He's gentle, but he doesn't baby her. He lets her do all of the work.

When we're in Seth's truck, driving back to my van, I turn to him. "Jesus, Seth, she's coming back from a major *stroke*, and she's so young."

"I know," he says softly. "And she's kicking ass."

"Were they dating before her stroke?"

"No. She was married at the time. After the stroke, the prick took off because it was too much for him to handle."

"What a douche."

"Gage took the rehab job, and the dating part has been slow-going. But he loves her. It's written all over him."

"I could see it too. He's sweet with her but doesn't do everything for her. He's a good balance for her."

Seth glances over at me, then back to the road. "Are you going to stay at your van tonight?"

"What are my options?" I smile when he cocks an eyebrow.

"You know I'd rather have you with me."

I slide my hand into his and hold on tight. Are we moving fast? Yes. But do I want to slow down?

No.

No, I don't.

"I'll pack a bag."

"Bring the whole van, Remi."

I'm quiet for a moment, thinking about it. I'm not canceling my spot at the RV park. I'm just bringing it out to Seth's so it's not sitting empty.

That's all.

"Okay."

He kisses my hand as he pulls next to the van.

CHAPTER 11

~SETH~

"*I* thought Troy was supposed to muck?" I lean on the shovel and wipe my face with my sleeve as my father spreads fresh hay in the stalls I've just cleaned.

"He's with your grandma again today," Dad replies. "I know it's time for him to move back home now, but I don't have the heart to make him."

I sigh and stare at the floor. When my grandpa died last year, it sent us all into a tailspin. We all hurt and are *still* grieving for the patriarch of our family.

He left us much too soon.

But my little brother Troy has been struggling the most and has refused to leave my grandmother's house, aside from the one night he stayed with me. He insists that he doesn't want her to be alone.

It's heartbreaking and sweet at the same time.

"Sometimes the other kids take a turn," Dad says. "But Troy's really been adamant to stay with her lately."

"She's not far from us," I remind Dad. "She's five minutes down the road. And I know she could move in with you and Mom if she wanted to. You have plenty of space in the big house."

"I'm aware of all of that," he says. "Mom wants to stay at her place. She's happy there."

I shrug and start on the next stall.

"Speaking of flinging shit around," I begin, "did Sarah talk to you about Kensie?"

"What? No."

I poke my head out of the stall again and find my father staring at me with wide eyes and a baffled expression. "Where did she come up with Kensie's name?"

"She's been doing a family tree for school. The kids were kind of upset, but I explained things, and they calmed down. Sarah said she has questions for you, so she'll probably bring it up at some point."

"Damn. Okay, thanks for the warning."

"She's dead, by the way. Kensie."

His head comes up again, and his eyes narrow. "How?"

"Murdered. The same idiot she was with when she dropped me off here killed her about six years ago."

His face doesn't change much. He doesn't seem sad. He doesn't even look particularly angry.

"And how are *you*?" he finally asks.

I shrug a shoulder. "I was curious, so I did some digging to find out how it all went down. Honestly, I wasn't particularly surprised. And I'm not sad. I'm not...anything. It was like I was reading an article about a stranger. Because that's what she was to me. But I found out during my research that she was arrested for whoring herself out, and that made me feel...I don't know, pity, I guess. She could have had a good life with you. Instead, she threw it all in the toilet and ended up a drug-addicted hooker."

"She was an angry person, Seth," Dad says. "Always. She never would have had a good life with me because nothing made her happy. And I'm not saying that in a spiteful way."

"I know. It's just the truth. She *was* unhappy. And she was mean. I'm not saying she got what was coming to her, but—" I shrug. "It didn't shock me that it ended like that for her."

"I'm not surprised either, honestly. You're not her. You know that, right? You're *nothing* like her, Seth."

"I know. I know that, Dad. Sometimes, especially that first year that I came to live here, I thought I was like her because I was so angry all the time. But then I figured out that I was mad because of her, not because I *am* her. She was a shitty mom, and I'm grateful that she was because it brought me here, with you and the mother who showed me what being a mom is all about. With Uncle Josh and Aunt Cara, and all of your crazy kids. If she'd kept me, well, I'd probably be in jail or dead. So, I pity her, and I hope she's found some peace."

Dad walks to me and pulls me in for a hug, patting my back. "I'm so fucking proud of you, buddy."

Instead of the life of physical and sexual abuse that I lived when I was with Kensie, *this* is what I have here in Montana. A father who isn't afraid to hug me and tell me he's proud of me.

I'll never tell him everything that happened when he was deployed, and I was with the woman who gave birth to me. It would tear him apart, and there's no need to do that to him.

I have my family and this ranch, and that was the best therapy I could have asked for.

"I know I'm your favorite," I say when he lets go, and as I intended, I make him laugh. "I love you, Dad."

He nods. "I know. I love you, too. I'll handle Sarah, and any of the others if they ask. Why don't you take the rest of the day off? Go find that pretty girl you've been seeing."

I grin. "She *is* pretty, isn't she?"

"Are you going to bring her to dinner tonight?"

"I was planning to."

"Good. I'll see you later, then."

"I can stay and finish the stalls."

"There are only two left, and Louie should be back with Josh in a bit. We've got this."

"Okay, but you can text me if you need me."

"You know, we ran this place just fine when you were a kid."

I laugh and put my shovel away. "But it's so much more fun now that I'm all grown up."

The drive over to my house doesn't take long, but I go even slower than usual so I can shake off the conversation I just had with my dad before seeing Remi. I don't like to dwell on what happened before I was eleven. And I usually don't. I haven't in years.

When I left this morning, Remi was sleeping soundly in my bed. She didn't even crack one of those beautiful eyes open when I kissed her goodbye.

But it's after seven now, so my guess is she'll be awake.

When I come around the bend that leads to my house, I see I'm not wrong. Remi is wrapped in a blanket, huddled up on the porch swing, a mug of steaming coffee clutched in her hands.

She grins as I park and then climb the steps toward her.

"Good morning," she says, her eyes still heavy with sleep.

"'Morning. You must have slept well."

"Like the dead," she confirms and sips her coffee. "Do you have a lot of work today?"

"Actually, no. My dad just gave me the rest of the day off. Do you have something in mind?"

"I haven't ridden a horse in a long time. Do you think we could do that today?"

141

I grin and reach for the mug she offers, taking a sip. "I just happen to know where we can get a couple of horses."

"How convenient."

I pass back the mug. "I need a quick shower, and then we can head to the barn."

"Don't use all the hot water."

"Come on, we'll conserve water and take a shower together."

"THIS IS STARFIRE," I say as I nuzzle the horse's muzzle. She nudges me affectionately and lets me drape the bridle over her head. "She's a sweetheart and is the most patient horse we have."

"She's so pretty." Remi rubs her hand confidently over the horse's flank, then walks to her head to talk to her. "Do you mind if I ride you today, sweet girl? I'll be nice to you, I promise."

Starfire nods and roots around Remi's hands, looking for an apple.

"I'll be on Magic. She's my horse. We should be ready to go here in about ten minutes."

Remi helps me with the saddles, and then we're off, riding through the pasture to the other side of the ranch, where some of my favorite places are.

"It's a nice day," Remi says as she takes a deep

breath. "The leaves on all of the trees have turned already."

"I bet we're in for a harsh winter."

"Why do you say that?"

"The leaves are falling now, and there has been a lot of snow in the higher elevations already."

"I hope we get a *ton* of snow," she says with a smile. "I'm excited for it."

"I'm not ready. We have a lot of winterizing work that needs to be done here on the ranch before winter can settle in. We have to move cattle to lower elevations so they don't freeze to death, and get other animals inside. It's a process."

"I never even thought of it that way," she murmurs. "Never a dull moment working a ranch, huh?"

"Never," I agree with a smile. "So, that spot over there is the best sledding hill on the property. I only broke my arm once."

She lets out a surprised laugh. "How many bones have you broken out here?"

"Well, I broke my ankle the first summer I lived here. Poor Aunt Cara. She was with me, and she still feels guilty for that one. Whenever I want to soften her up for something, I tell her my ankle is giving me fits, and she'll give me pretty much anything I want."

"You're a manipulator," Remi accuses.

I laugh and shrug. "She knows what I'm doing. Anyway, there was the ankle, my arm on the sledding hill, and once I broke my nose when I fell off a horse we were breaking."

"Ouch."

"Yeah, I saw stars for a week. How about you? With as adventurous as you are, you've definitely broken something."

"I broke my collarbone once. Fell off my bike in Moab. Dislocated the shoulder. No other major injuries. Just scrapes and bumps here and there."

I point to the tree to our left. "That's sort of a big deal in our family."

"Are those carvings in it?"

"Yeah, going back to my great-great-great-grand-parents, the men have carved their initials with those of the women they love. It's tradition. And you can see how the tree has grown, and the older initials are higher up."

"That's super cool. How long has your family been on this property?"

"Oh, geez." I blow out a breath and think back. "At least a hundred and fifty years. We own just over fifty thousand acres."

"Seth, this is more than a family business. This is a legacy."

"Yeah." I smile as I nod at her. "It's pretty cool. Oh, there are some cabins over that way where hunters can stay during hunting season. We host some people, and others just come and stay in the cabins on their own."

"Another income stream?"

"You have to use what you have, and we have a lot here, honestly."

She nods and seems to be enjoying the view, which makes me happy. Something catches her eye, and she points off to the right.

"Is that a cemetery?"

"It is."

"Can we go look?"

I raise a brow. "Sure, if you want."

"I want."

We turn the horses that way, and when we reach the wrought iron fence that surrounds the graveyard, we hop off the horses and drop the reins. The horses won't go far and even start to graze as I open the gate for Remi.

"This is *so* cool. You have your own cemetery."

There are several dozen headstones placed throughout the area, starting back by the trees.

"The oldest ones are back there." I point them out to her, and we start to wander through the graveyard. "The kids think this place is creepy, but I've never felt that way out here. It's peaceful."

"Some of these headstones go back to the late 1800s." She stops and crosses her arms over her chest as she reads one of the headstones. "Clifford King. Born 1842. Died 1889. Loved his land, God, and family."

I nod. "He was the first King on this property. And his initials, along with his wife's, are on that tree."

145

She slowly moves up and down the rows of gravestones, reading each of them.

"This one is newer."

"That's my grandpa," I reply and stare at the gray stone.

Jeffrey King
1950-2020
Beloved

"Heart attack," I continue. "But he didn't suffer, and that's the important thing."

She slides her hand into mine and gives it a squeeze. "You were close?"

"Yeah." I glance down at her. "He was the best."

We walk a little farther and she points to the simple wooden cross next to my grandpa. "What's this?"

"That's Thor." I smile softly. "I got him that first summer I came to the ranch. He was the best dog ever. Goofy and big and loyal. He died a few years ago, and I put him here because he was part of the family."

"And now you have Captain," she says with a smile. "I take it you're a Marvel fan."

"Isn't everyone?"

She laughs and tugs me next to her. "Where has Cap been?"

"At the big house with the kids. He's mine, but I share custody."

She rests her head on my biceps and takes a long, deep breath.

"This ranch is special, Seth. Thank you for showing it to me today."

"You're welcome, but we didn't even cover half of it." I kiss her head, and we turn to walk back to the horses. "There are swimming holes and even a natural cellar out here that they used to use to dry out meat a hundred years ago."

"You know this place like the back of your own hand, don't you?"

"Of course."

"I don't think I've ever lived anywhere that meant as much to me as this does to your family."

I close the gate behind us and then turn her into my arms, tipping her chin up so I can brush my lips over hers.

"You'll find your place, Remi. It's out there, waiting for you."

It's here.

I want to say it out loud, but she's not ready for that. She's not ready to hear that I plan to marry her. To make a life with her.

But that time will come.

"Oh, by the way," I say as I help her up onto her horse. "It's Sunday, and that usually means that we have dinner at the big house. Are you up for it?"

"Sure." She smiles over at me as I settle in my own saddle. "I've already met them all once. It'll be a nice, quiet evening."

I snort. "My family isn't quiet, sugar. Nice? Yes. And

the food is out of this world. But they're not quiet. You'll meet my grandma. She always bakes the dessert, and she makes the best damn pie in the world."

"I like pie." She nods. "And, honestly, I like to cook. A lot. Mind if I borrow your kitchen one of these days?"

"Honey, you can use my kitchen anytime you like, as long as I get to eat whatever you make."

"I make enough for an army."

"Yeah. You're going to fit in just fine."

CHAPTER 12

~REMI~

"*J*'m going to meet his family." I cradle the phone close to my mouth.

"Why are you whispering?" Annie asks on the other end of the phone, also whispering loudly.

"Because he's in the other room, and I'm acting nonchalant in front of him, but I'm chalant as all fuck, Annie."

She giggles, and I scowl.

"It's not funny!"

"Of course, not," she whispers. "Wait, why am *I* whispering? Okay, tell me what's happening. Lay it all out for me."

"He invited me to Sunday night dinner with his whole family. Even his grandma. The. Whole. Family."

"Oh, I like Nancy so much. You'll love her."

"You're not helping."

"What do you want me to say? I mean, I'm trying to

be a good friend here, Remi, but I don't know why this is a bad thing. If you don't want to go, just say so. Tell him you have other plans or something."

"I don't have other plans." I chew on my thumbnail and will my stomach to stop roiling. "I made it seem like it's no big deal earlier when we were out on the horses, but holy shit, Annie. He wants me to have dinner with his whole family. Isn't that a thing? Am I ready for it to be a thing?"

Annie sighs, and I know I'm being that frustrating friend that wants to have the situation solved miraculously. But I can't help it. This has never happened to me before.

"Remi. You spend more time with him than not. You're sleeping with him."

"I never said—"

"A woman knows these things. I saw the way you lit up from the inside out when he stopped into the deli on Friday. I hate to break it to you, but this is already a *thing*. But if you don't want to go, don't go."

"It's not that I don't want to go." I check to make sure Seth is still in the kitchen. "I do. Sort of. But damn it, I'm nervous. This is his whole family. His parents, siblings, and his grandmother."

"And probably his aunt and uncle and their kids, too."

"Holy shit, Annie."

"I know, not helping. Okay, you need to take a deep

breath, honey. I suspect you're not close to your family the way that Seth is."

"Totally not. Not even close. My mother can't even remember my birthday."

"Wait, what? Remi, when is your birthday?"

"Focus, Annie."

"Right. Go. Enjoy it. Worry about the rest later."

"That's it? Those are your words of wisdom?"

"You're overthinking," she says with laughter in her voice. "Go enjoy that sexy man of yours. Call me if you need me."

"Okay. Thanks. Bye."

I hang up and turn around, running right into a very solid, very hard chest.

"Holy shit! You scared me. You can't just sneak up on people like that, Seth. It's rude."

He's quiet, so I let my eyes travel up his chest, throat, and to his face. His eyes are narrowed. His jaw tight.

"What?"

"You can just talk to me about this, you know."

I swallow hard. "Not really."

"Why?"

"Because I don't want to hurt your feelings, Seth. I don't want to turn down your invitation. I want to go with you."

"But you have to call a friend to get up the guts? That tells me you don't want to go. And if that's the case, you need to say so."

"Why do you want me there?"

There. I said it. It's out in the universe now.

Seth licks his lips and moves in closer, nudging me back until I'm flush against the wall. His hands slide over my hips, and his nose skims my cheek.

"Because I like being with you. I want you to hang out with the people I like best. You don't have anything to worry about, Rem. I'll be right there with you."

"What if they don't like me?" I hate the shakiness in my voice.

"What's not to like? Have you *met* you?"

I smile a little and feel the heat ripple through me and my nipples pucker as those magical hands of his slide up to my rib cage.

"I mean, I *am* pretty cool."

"The coolest," he agrees. "If you hate it, we'll leave. No questions asked. No harm, no foul."

"It's easy to say that now—"

"Look at me, damn it."

My eyes fly up to his, the hardness in his voice surprising me.

"I don't say shit I don't mean. We don't have time for games. Listen to me carefully. If you're not comfortable tonight, you just say so, and we'll leave. I won't be mad. I won't punish you with the silent treatment or guilt-trip you. We'll just go, and move on with our lives until you *are* comfortable. Okay?"

"Yeah. Okay."

He kisses my forehead, takes a deep breath, and then backs away with my hand clenched in his.

"Good. Let's go."

His stride is purposeful as he leads me through the house and out to his truck. He's on a mission, and it seems that mission is to take me to a family dinner.

It's kind of sweet, really. My stomach is still tight, and I'm nervous as all hell, but he's sweet, and in the brief moments that I met his family, they were nice.

It's going to be fine.

The drive over to his parents' house doesn't take long, and before I know it, we're pulling to a stop in front of a big, red farmhouse that has clearly been the focal point of this property for a very long time.

"How old is this house?" I ask him when he turns off the engine, and we sit staring at it.

He seems to exhale in relief, as if he'd been holding his breath, expecting me to tell him to take me back.

"The original house was built in 1870, but it's been renovated and added on to so much over the years, I couldn't tell you what's original."

"Interesting. I like old houses."

I open my door and hop out of the truck, then meet Seth at the bottom of the steps of the porch and take his hand. I'm proud that my hand isn't shaking.

"Let's go have dinner," I say with a smile.

"You sure you're good?" he asks and looks closely at my face, checking for any sign of trepidation.

"I'm great. I mean it." And I really do mean it. I had

a few moments of insecurity, but Seth reassured me. Bolstered my confidence. I'm just nervous because I'll be surrounded by people I don't know. But I'll get past it. I've been in these situations before.

We climb the steps of the porch, and Seth walks right through the door without knocking.

We're greeted with big smiles and hugs, words of welcome. Seth's mom, Jillian, wraps her arm around my waist and leads me toward the kitchen.

"Come, have a glass of wine and chat with us," she suggests.

"I could use a glass of wine."

"I'll come, too," Seth says, but his mom shakes her head.

"Your dad was looking for you a few minutes ago. He and the other guys are out trying to fix your brother's snowmobile. Don't worry, we won't scare her off."

With his mother looking on, Seth leans over and kisses my cheek, then whispers in my ear, "Don't run. I'm right outside."

I watch him walk off and then smile at Jillian.

"Let's get that wine," she suggests with a laugh.

I rarely drink. But I think I need just a little something to take the edge off.

"Red or white?" Cara asks when I walk into the kitchen.

"Surprise me," I reply.

"We're just going casual tonight," Cara says as she fills some glasses with white wine and passes one to me. "We're laying out a taco bar so everyone can pick on it all evening. We're usually casual around here unless it's a holiday."

"Yeah, then we break out the linen napkins," Jillian says with a wink. "The kids are upstairs playing video games or on their phones. Or something."

"I'm right here." A teenager that I recognize from my first afternoon at the deli speaks up at the sink where he's rinsing off vegetables.

"And you're my favorite," Jillian assures him. "Miles, have you met Remi?"

He smiles over at me. "Yeah, we checked her out at the deli last week."

I raise a brow. "So you didn't just stop by for an after-school cookie?"

That cocky smile is just like his other brother's. "The cookie was great. I could have eaten six more. But we all stopped by to see you."

I narrow my eyes and sip my wine. "So, all of the kids you were with—?"

"My sibs and cousins," he confirms.

"No wonder Annie laughed," I mutter and shake my head.

"They didn't mean any harm," a redheaded woman says as she walks out of the pantry, carrying taco shells and cans of beans and corn. "I'm Lauren, by the way."

"I remember," I say. "I know they didn't. It was just funny, especially to Annie, because I think all of Seth's family stopped in at some point that day. She got a real kick out of it."

"The Kings are a nosy bunch."

I turn at the voice and see an older woman just slipping out of her jacket. Her eyes are keen on me as she takes me in.

"You must be Nancy King," I say with a smile. "Your grandson is smitten with you, you know."

"All of them are," she replies with a soft smile. "And I with them. You're a beautiful girl, Remi."

I feel my cheeks heat. "Thanks. You're all so pretty and nice. You're a little overwhelming, you know that?"

"It's just because there's so many of us," Jillian insists and shares a look with her mother-in-law.

Well, I can make it awkward and just stand here, or I can make it fun.

"How can I help?" I ask and set my wine aside. "I'm a good cook, and I know my way around a kitchen. This one is beautiful, by the way."

"Thanks," Jillian says. "We did some work on it about five years ago. You can get into that cabinet there and pull down some bowls for all of this stuff."

For the next thirty minutes, we bustle about the kitchen, and I watch as they all fall into a rhythm that they've clearly perfected over the course of many years together as a family.

"How is Lauren related?" I ask when there's a break in the conversation. "I know that Cara is married to Josh."

"I'm married to Ty, Jillian's brother," Lauren says with a smile. "Our daughter is Layla. She was likely with Miles and the others last week."

"She was," Miles confirms and stirs the fresh salsa that he just made entirely from scratch. "We were all together."

"So, Ty's the only one I haven't met then," I reply, then look around in surprise when they all giggle. "What?"

"Ty went in that day, too," Lauren confesses.

"Have you never met one of Seth's girlfriends before or something?" I take a sip of my now-warm wine.

"No," Jillian replies. "He's never really talked with us about women. I know he's dated, don't get me wrong. But until you, he's kept that part of his life relatively private. At least from us. He might talk to Zack and Josh about it more."

I blink at her, then finish the glass of wine in two gulps.

"I suppose we're not doing a very good job of putting you at ease," Nancy says and pats me on the shoulder. "I told you, we're all a nosy bunch, especially when it comes to our kids. But I like you, and I can see why Seth does, too."

"Why?" I ask before I can stop myself, then cover my mouth with my hand and feel my eyes widen in horror. "Sorry. That's the wine talking."

"You're smart," Nancy says without blinking. "And

157

kind. And when you smile, you light up the room. It's no wonder that my grandson can't take his eyes off you."

I clear my throat and smile gratefully at Cara when she pours me just a smidge more wine.

"I'm cut off after this," I inform her. "I'm a lightweight."

"Me, too," she says with a wink.

CHAPTER 13

~REMI~

"So, where do you see yourself in five years?"

I choke on the chip I just bit into and then blink away the tears that formed from it and into the eyes of a very serious middle-schooler.

"Is this a job interview?" I ask him.

"Maybe." Troy shrugs but doesn't look away and doesn't laugh.

"Five years is a long time."

"Okay, where do you see yourself in *one* year?" he persists.

"Hmm. Probably still traveling in my van, exploring the country."

"Not in Cunningham Falls? What will you do for work?"

I grin at him. "Maybe I'll still be here. I like working at the deli."

"Can you score free cookies?"

I laugh and reach for another chip. "Probably. What kind is your favorite?"

"Peanut butter," he says. "The oatmeal is good, too."

"What about kids?" This comes from Layla, who's sitting to my right. Somehow, Miles talked me into coming into the living room with all of the kids after we ate dinner, and now it's like I'm at the Spanish Inquisition.

"I like kids."

"Do you want some?" Kimberly asks.

I'm shocked that I can remember all of their names.

"I...uh...Maybe. If I met the right guy and we decided to have kids together, I would be up for it. But I don't know if I'd be a very good mom."

"Why?" Miles frowns at me. "You're nice enough."

I laugh and shrug a shoulder. "Well, thanks. I don't know, I think kids are a big decision, and I'm not really in a position to think about it."

"Because you're not married?" Sarah asks.

"Well, yeah. I live in my van. It's not really the right place to raise a kid or two, you know?"

"Yeah, you'll definitely have to move out of the van if you have kids," Troy says.

"Let's change this subject," I suggest and look over to the dining room, where Seth is watching me with a wide grin on his impossibly handsome face. "Why aren't you in here answering questions?"

"Because I already did that last weekend," he informs me.

"I feel like I should have brought my resume with me tonight."

"Oh, do you have one you can email us?" Kim asks.

"No." I shake my head. "I won't email you my resume."

"It's okay," Kim continues, "my dad is an attorney. We can do a background check."

"What did you do?" I hear Seth ask his dad.

Zack leans back in his chair and smiles proudly. "My dirty work."

This family is just...hilarious. And welcoming. Warm. *Kind.* They laugh together, and they genuinely like being together. They clearly protect one another.

It's unlike anything I've ever experienced before. I'm not nervous about being here anymore. They have done nothing but make me feel included, even with this interrogation by the teens.

But now there's a new little seed of doubt planted in the center of my belly.

I don't belong here.

"Okay, there will be no background check," Seth says as he walks into the room and sits next to me. "Did you guys know that Remi was on TV?"

"Of course," Sarah replies, almost insulted that Seth would think otherwise. "We've watched her. It's so cool."

"Dad won't let me ride my bike downhill," Troy mutters.

"You ride it downhill all the time," Seth says.

"Not down the mountains, with jumps and obstacles," Troy insists.

"You'll break your neck," Jillian calls from the kitchen. "I like keeping you around."

"I won't break my neck," Troy says with a stubborn frown.

"Personally, I think that some of the things you do here on the ranch are way cooler than downhill biking," I inform him.

"Like what?"

"Riding horses, fly-fishing, riding snowmobiles, ATVs, hiking. Just to name a few."

"Those are fun, but not *thrill-seeking*," he insists.

"I don't know," Josh puts in. "It was pretty thrilling when I ran into that mountain lion when I was fishing last week."

"Remi and I ran smack dab into a grizzly when we were stuck up in the park," Seth adds. "I don't recommend that you guys go out and find wildlife, though. Please don't do that."

The conversation ebbs and flows from my own experiences to the different animals the kids have seen, and after everyone has helped clean up, and it's time to go, I'm folded in for hugs.

"Please come back again soon," Jillian says.

"Thank you," I reply, not committing to another family dinner quite yet.

Troy and Nancy leave together, hand in hand. I see

the others share a glance when the door closes behind them.

"Soon," Zack mutters. "I'll talk with him soon."

"Thanks again for inviting me," I say with a wave. "Have a good night."

Seth and I walk out into the cold Montana night and hop into his truck. He fires up the engine, and I turn to look out the window.

I feel…lonely. How could I just spend three hours with so many people and leave feeling lonely?

Because I don't belong here. I don't know how to act or what to say. I don't know what it is to be around people who show so much love. Who *want* to be together and actually look sad when the night is over.

I've never had that.

Maybe it's too much, too fast. Maybe I just need a little time away from Seth to sort through my feelings and put some distance between us.

When Seth comes to a stop in front of his house, I hop out of the truck and walk inside behind him.

He's whistling.

He's happy.

"You know what? I think I'll gather my things and head back to the campsite tonight."

He stops and turns with a frown. "Why?"

"Well, you know, I've been here for a while now, and I don't want to impose. I really should just get out of your hair for a few days."

"You're not in my hair." He props his hands on his hips. "What's wrong?"

"Nothing." I swallow hard and shake my head. "Nothing's wrong."

"Did someone say something mean to you at my parents' place when I was outside?"

"No, not at all. Everyone was really nice. You're right, they're good people, Seth. And the food was fantastic."

"So, no one was mean, and you had a good time, but you're going to leave?"

I lick my lips, frustrated. "I know it might be hard for someone like you to understand the words *I need time alone*, what with you always having fifty-eight people around at any given time. But I want to go."

I grab my purse and turn to the door. I can get my other things later. Right now, I just want to *go*.

"Stop. If you leave right now, I swear to God, I'll spank your ass."

I turn slowly and stare at him as if he's lost his mind. "I beg your pardon?"

"I didn't stutter." He crosses his arms over his chest. "We're going to have this out, and then, if you're pissed and can't stand the sight of me, you can go."

"You can't just keep me here."

He sighs in frustration and pushes his hands through his hair, paces away, and then holds those hands out at his sides.

"Why are you so frustrating? Just *talk* to me,

goddamn it! Tell me why, after a nice evening with my family, you're ready to run away."

"I'm not running away."

"Then what exactly are you doing, Remi? Because it looks to me like you're running."

"I don't belong here!" His face loses all emotion at my outburst. "You have this amazing family, with so many great people in it who love you so much, Seth. There was so much love in that house, I expected to see little cartoon hearts floating in the air."

His jaw clenches.

"I can't tell you the last time my mother told me she loved me. I don't remember. She called me a few days ago to wish me happy birthday. Only, it *wasn't* my damn birthday. I know we've already discussed my family and how different it is from yours, so you should understand that I don't have any kind of compass or roadmap for dealing with this."

"You're telling me that you've never been around anyone who showed you affection?"

"Not without an ulterior motive." I shake my head vigorously when he takes a step toward me. "No, I don't need pity. I'm not hurt or whatever. I'm saying that I don't know how to be around people like that. I don't know how to trust it. And it overwhelms me."

"Baby—"

"Don't placate me."

"Okay, that's enough." His face is mutinous now, his hands balled into fists at his sides. "Don't fucking tell me how to feel or react to you, Remi. I thought you were having a good time. You laughed, you talked, and you seemed comfortable."

"It's not that I was *un*comfortable."

"Then I don't know what to say or do to make it any better for you," he says at last. "You have a shitty family. A shit mom. And I know what that's like, so let me assure you, I didn't trust the love that those people so freely showed me at first, either. But I can tell you this. They don't want squat from you, except maybe that you aren't an asshole or something. But I know you're not, so that's covered."

"I feel like an asshole."

"I refuse to let you run away from me every time things get hard, or heavy, or uncomfortable."

"I do things alone," I inform him. "That's who I am."

"I don't buy it."

"You don't have to. I'm *telling* you, this is who I am. Take it or leave it. I'm going back to the campsite."

I turn to leave, but Seth suddenly spins me to him and pins me to the door with my face in his hands and his lips hot on mine. He's pissed off, but he's not hurting me. He's intense.

Being with Seth is always intense, no matter what we're doing. My feelings for him are all-consuming. As if they've permeated the very essence of who I am.

My hands dive into his thick, dark hair, and he boosts me up so I can wrap my legs around his waist.

"Don't you even think of fucking leaving me," he

growls against my neck before biting and then sucking my skin.

"That's not creepy at all."

He braces one hand against the wall and tips his forehead against mine as he chuckles.

"*Not* in a creepy way."

He carries me through the house as if it's effortless, straight to his bed. He gently lays me down and crawls over me to nibble my lips.

"Don't you get it?" His mouth is against mine as he speaks. "You're everything, Remi. You're fucking everything."

And then there are no words as he unzips my jeans and slides his hand inside, under my panties, and presses a finger inside of me.

I arch my back and tear at his shirt, needing to feel his skin against mine.

He pulls his hand away long enough to strip us both bare, and then I'm swamped by desire. By the absolute fierceness in him as he takes what he needs and gives back more than I ever thought possible.

My God, I love him. I love him so much that it paralyzes me with fear. I don't know how to love. Not really. And Seth deserves so much of it.

I feel my eyes fill with tears as he rolls to the side, gasping for breath, and then kisses the hand he's had pinned above my head. When his eyes find mine, they widen in horror.

"Oh, baby, I'm sorry. I didn't mean to hurt you, or make you stay, or do anything—"

"No." I cup his face in my hands and hurry to reassure him. "No, you didn't do anything wrong. I promise."

"Then what are the tears for?"

I swallow, and I know that I have to tell him the truth because anything else would be a lie. It would be a game.

"I'm so scared," I whisper.

"I've got you. You're safe here."

"I know." He's done nothing but show me that he'll protect me at all costs since the day he saved me in those mountains. "I'm scared because what I feel for you is so big, so deep, that I'm terrified I'll screw it all up."

"I'm in love with you," he admits without hesitation. As if the words flow as freely as the river on his land. "I think I have been since I first saw you. If I'd have let you walk out of here tonight, full of doubt and uncertainty, I would have lost you, Remi, and that's just not possible."

My eyes fill again. Have I ever felt so important, so *vital* to another person?

No.

And that's what scares me and also fills me with joy.

"Wow."

His lips tip up into a smile. "Yeah. Wow."

"The thing is, I—" I lick my lips. "I love you, too."

"I know."

I raise an eyebrow. "Oh, really?"

"I figure that's the only thing that would make you want to run for the hills."

I chuckle. "Just because you kept me here with your sexy ways doesn't mean I'm not still scared, you know."

"Oh, I'm terrified," he says casually and pulls me against him for a snuggle. "But the way I like to think of it, we'll just figure it out as we go. You don't have a roadmap because there isn't one, Rem."

"So, we just *wing* it?"

"I guess so."

"Well, that's just stupid. I'm a planner, Seth."

"Says the woman who's been living by the seat of her pants in a van for several months."

I narrow my eyes. "But I *planned* it."

"You planned the spontaneity?"

"Yes. Sort of. Stop confusing me."

He laughs and rolls me onto my back, then kisses me long and slow in the way I've come to love so much.

CHAPTER 14

~SETH~

"*I'll make you something to eat.*" *Mom smiles and ruffles my hair. I've gotten used to letting her touch me whenever she wants without flinching or moving away. I'm safe here at our ranch in Montana, and Mom makes me stuff to eat anytime I want. I can ask for food and actually get it.*

And I'm hungry now.

"Can I have a sandwich?"

"Sure, do you want some chips, too?"

I grin at her. "Yeah. And maybe you can cut it in that cool way that you do."

The best thing my dad ever did was marry Jillian. And now that he's home, and we're a family, things aren't bad. My other mom lied to me and made me believe that my dad doesn't love me.

But that's not true.

I turn to watch the TV, but suddenly, everything is

different. I'm not in the ranch house. This is the gross old apartment in Texas.

"You think you can just be lazy?"

I spin and freeze in fear when Kensie, my other mom, sneers at me.

"I'm just hungry."

"You're always hungry. You're nothing but a pain in my ass. No wonder your dad left and didn't look back. Just look at you. You're worthless."

No, I'm not.

I want to yell at her that I'm not worthless, but if I talk back, it'll only get worse.

"Yes, ma'am." *I lower my head and look at the floor. Why am I here? Where's the ranch? Where's Jillian?*

"You can go hungry, you little shit. I'm not wasting my hard-earned money on food for you."

She has sex with men in exchange for money. Sometimes, she even forgets I'm here in the room with her when she does it. It makes my tummy hurt, and I want to run away so I don't have to see it anymore.

And, sometimes, it's worse than that. Sometimes, she lets the men do things to me. That's when it's worst of all. But it's over. I'm at the ranch.

Where is the ranch?

"Why don't you let me have a go at him?"

No. Oh God, no.

I shake my head vigorously as beefy, mean hands grab at me.

171

"Don't you tell me no," Kensie says. Her breath stinks. It smells like cigarettes and beer. *"You be nice, you hear me?"*

"I don't want to." I whimper. *"Please, I don't want to."*

"Seth."

I jump out of the bed and run for the bathroom, splash cold water on my face, and will the nightmare to dissipate.

Jesus. Jesus Christ, this hasn't happened in years. My stomach roils, and I'm dizzy.

And suddenly so damn hungry.

I know it's all in my head, but I always wake from these dreams feeling hungrier than ever.

"Seth."

I lift my gaze and meet Remi's in the mirror.

"I'm okay."

"No, you're not." She steps to me and tentatively lays her hand on my arm. "Honey, you're not okay."

Without thinking, I pull her against me and bury my nose in her hair, breathing her in. Her sweet smell, her warmth, her *goodness.* I soak her in and cling to her as she pushes the sickness out of me.

"Come on," she urges and leads me back to the bed. "Let's just breathe for a minute."

"I'm fine. I'll be okay."

"I know you will, but that was a hell of a nightmare. You were thrashing and fighting."

I look down at her for the first time and see a bruise on her shoulder. "Jesus, what did I do to you?"

"You just pushed me aside when I tried to touch you. It's my own fault. I know better than to do that."

"Oh my God." I back away from her, not touching her at all. "I *hurt* you."

"Hey, look at me, Seth. Damn it, look at me."

My eyes meet hers.

"I'm fine. I just bruise easily, that's all. You didn't hurt me."

"Bullshit. I put a mark on you, Remi. That's not acceptable. Not ever. I don't care if I *am* living through hell. That can't happen."

She narrows her eyes. "Tell me about the nightmare."

"No." My voice is flat. "I don't remember it."

"Now I call bullshit."

"It doesn't matter."

"Oh, it matters. I can see all over your face that it matters. You're white as a ghost, and if you grasp that blanket any tighter, you'll rip it." She rubs her hand up and down my thigh. "It's okay."

I close my eyes. I wish this part of me didn't exist. That my dad had left her years before, and that the only memories I have are of this ranch.

But it's here. And if I want to have any kind of future with this amazing woman, I need to tell her so she can decide for herself if my baggage is something she wants to deal with.

"Kensie, my biological mother, was pretty awful. You already know that."

She nods but doesn't say anything.

"She liked it when I was hungry. When I begged for food. For anything, really. Because it made her feel in control, and she enjoyed withholding stuff from me."

Remi blinks, and I see the rage in her eyes, but she stays quiet.

"So, in the dream, I was a kid. Around the age I was when I came here. Maybe a little younger. And it started in the kitchen of the big house, the way it was when I was little, and Jillian offered to make me a sandwich. I remember thinking that the best thing my dad ever did was marry her." My eyes meet Remi's. "And I was right. Anyway, I turned away, and then I was in Texas with Kensie, and she was taunting me with food. Saying mean things, the way she used to. And that's all."

Remi tilts her head to the side. "I don't think that's all. Just tell me, Seth. I can handle it."

I chew my lip and then let the words tumble out of my mouth.

"She liked to let her men have a go at me."

Remi gasps, but I keep talking.

"They'd pay her more if they could touch me. Sometimes, that's all it was, some touching. Other times, it was rape."

"Oh, babe."

Remi climbs into my lap and wraps her arms around my shoulders, then buries her face in my neck.

"Before I was eleven, I'd seen more than any kid ever should. I'd seen drugs and way, way too much sex.

Mostly, she just forgot about me, you know? Forgot to feed me, forgot that I was in the room when she let a guy go at her. But when the dude took an interest in *me*, she didn't say no. Ever."

"I'm so sorry." Remi presses a kiss to my cheek. "Seth, did your dad want to kill her when he found out?"

"I've never told him. I've never told anyone."

She pulls back and stares at me in surprise. "What? Why?"

"Because it was over." I shrug. "Because I was here and safe, and she was gone. I confided in Cara a little that first year, and she was very understanding. She was my safe person for a while, you know?"

"Yeah. I know."

"I felt guilty. I thought that if they knew the whole truth, they might be disgusted and make me leave. And leaving, being cast away from here, was my worst nightmare. I'd do *anything* to not have to go back with Kensie. So I kept it to myself, and as time passed, and I knew that I didn't have to go hungry—for food or love —I relaxed. The nightmares were bad at first, but they lessened with time. I couldn't tell you the last time I had one."

"Why do you think you had one tonight?"

I blow out a breath. "I recently found out that Kensie's dead. She died a long time ago, but I hadn't heard. It's caused some conversations with my dad, with my siblings, and I guess it's probably been swimming around in my head a bit. It's not like I'm sad that she's dead."

"Why would you be?" Remi's voice is fierce. "I want to wrap my hands around her throat myself and make her pay."

"She paid," I reply and kiss her forehead, then her lips. "She definitely paid for it. Like I said, I don't dream about her or what happened before. At least not often. But it could happen once in a while. And, damn it, I won't have you hurt because of it."

"Seriously, Seth, it startled me more than it hurt me. I hated hearing you cry out. You sounded scared and wounded, and I just wanted you to wake up. I'll be more careful if it happens again."

"You don't want to head for the hills?"

She stares up at me. "Why would I? Because you were abused? Raped? Hurt? That would make me an asshole, Seth. I just want you to be okay."

"There was a time I would have said that I don't deserve to be loved like this."

"That time is over. You have more love in a two-mile radius than I've ever seen in my life. You deserve it. Maybe more than anyone else. Now, are you hungry?"

"Why do you ask?"

"Because your stomach just growled. How about some middle-of-the-night pizza on the porch?"

"It's a date."

CHAPTER 15

~ REMI ~

"*H*i, Remi."

I look up from what I'm doing behind the deli counter and smile when I see Miles King walk up, his backpack slung over his shoulder, and a happy grin on his face.

"Well, hey there. How was school?"

"Meh, fine, I guess. I was hoping I could score some cookies."

I laugh and turn to grab the box of cookies and scones that I've had ready for him after school for the past month, ever since that first family dinner I went to. I always tell him to share with the other kids when he gets home, but I suspect he eats more than his share.

I don't even care. Miles has wormed his way into a soft spot in my heart.

"Here you go, handsome. Be sure to share those."

He scoffs as if the reminder is an insult. "Duh. Of course, I share. They get at least one."

"You brat."

His smile is sly and satisfied as he slips out the door, headed for his car so he can go home for the day.

"I'd say you've managed to fit into the King family pretty seamlessly," Annie says when she walks out of the kitchen, wiping her hands on a towel. "That kid adores you."

"It's kind of mutual. I know I shouldn't have a favorite, but he's pretty great. They're all good kids."

"Is Troy still staying with Nancy?"

"He went home last weekend," I reply and wrap some bread that didn't sell to go in the day-old basket for tomorrow. "He wasn't happy about it, but Zack talked him into it. I think he'll still go stay with his grandma once or twice a week."

"That's okay. He loves her."

I nod and set the last loaf in the basket. When I turn around, Annie's holding a bouquet of flowers and a card.

"Happy birthday," she says with a smile. "It's not much, but it's something."

I stare at the flowers for a second and then take them from her and bury my nose in a rose. "These are gorgeous."

"Brooke down the street at the flower shop knows what she's doing," Annie says with a wink. "What did Seth get you?"

"Nothing that I'm aware of."

She blinks at me in confusion. "You *told* him it's your birthday, right?"

Guilt immediately sets in. "Uh."

"*Remi.*"

"How do I do that? Just casually, in the middle of a conversation, say, 'Oh, by the way, my birthday is at the end of October. Get me something nice.'? I can't do that."

"I'm calling him," Annie announces.

"Why? No. Don't call him."

"He will be so mad at you," she says.

"He doesn't have to know. It's no big deal. My family didn't make a fuss over birthdays."

"Yes. I remember you telling me that your mother is a piece of shit. So I looked at the copy of the driver's license you gave me so I didn't forget. And, Remi, Seth needs to know. I'm going to *text* him. Just casually mention that it's your birthday. Give the poor man a chance to do something nice for you. I'll just make it seem like I'm giving him a gentle reminder."

"Do you really think he'll be mad?"

"Hell, yes. I do."

"Okay, fine. That works."

My phone rings in my pocket, surprising me. No one ever calls me.

"I have to grab this. It's my agent."

Annie waves me off, and I take the call. "Hello?"

179

"Happy birthday, sweet pea," Roberta says in my ear. "Are you having a good day?"

"Yeah, I'm working, but I like this job."

"You have a *job*? Why don't I know about this, Rem? I'm supposed to book your gigs for you."

"Calm down, Bert. I'm working in a deli in small-town, USA. I'm not on a set."

"Oh. Really? Okay, then. Well, I have good news for you. I just booked you on a show."

"No. I told you, I'm retired from that."

"Just hear me out. It's not for a whole season, it's only one week, down in Moab. They're bringing back all of the original winners from previous seasons for a one-week challenge, and they'll announce the winner on live national TV."

"How long do I have to get in shape for it?"

And why am I even considering it? The idea doesn't excite me at all.

"Well, not much time. You have to be down there by Monday."

"Bert, it's *Friday.* I would have to leave on Sunday to be there on time. Maybe even tomorrow."

"I know, the timing sucks. A show just got canceled, and they need to fill the time slot for a week, and this is what they're going with. You'll only be gone for a week, Rem, and they'll pay you well for it."

My eyes widen at the number she rattles off. I could use six figures for my nest egg.

"One week." I turn and look at Annie, who's already

locked up for the day and is scrubbing the countertop. "I have a job here, you know."

"You can have three hours to decide. I have to give them a yes or no *today*."

"No pressure or anything." I roll my eyes. "I'll call you back."

She hangs up, and I turn to Annie. "Hey, Ann?"

"Yeah?"

"Would you be okay here next week if I had to take it off?"

Her gaze whips up to mine. "Are you okay? Is your family okay?"

"Everyone's fine, as far as I know." I relay the offer I just got from Bert. "I don't know if I want to go, so if you tell me I can't have the time off, it's totally okay."

"I'll be fine if you decide to go."

"Well, damn." My phone rings again. "I'm suddenly popular. Hello?"

"You didn't tell me that it's your birthday," Seth says in my ear. "I'm going to spank you for that later."

"Promises, promises."

"I'm taking you out for dinner tonight."

"Okay. Can we go to Ciao? I could go for some carbs. Not that I should, but it's my birthday, and sometimes a girl needs pasta."

"You can have whatever you want."

"Cool. Also, we need to talk, Seth."

"Sounds serious. You okay?"

"Yeah. I just need your opinion."

"Okay. I'll meet you at home in an hour, and then we'll get ready to go to dinner."

"Okay. See you soon."

I click off and turn to Annie. "I'll talk to Seth and see what he thinks. I'll keep you posted."

"That's fine with me. Go enjoy your birthday. Have some extra garlic bread for me, okay?"

"I can do that."

"YOU SHOULD GO." Seth leans back in his seat and pushes his empty plate away from him. "It's only a week, and you'll kick ass."

"I'm *not* in shape for a challenge show." I shake my head and swirl the last of my wine. "I should have been training for a month or more."

"You're in great shape."

"Yes, for everyday things. This isn't lifestyle fitness we're talking about here. I'll be climbing and jumping and all kinds of shit that takes strength. I'm so mad at her for calling me with just a few hours to decide."

"Do you get paid whether you're the first kicked off or the winner?"

"I'd get paid something. More the longer I'm there. And even more if I win."

"I'm not saying that it's about the money, I'm just curious."

"Seth, I've won so much money over the past seven

years, and I have a great financial guy. I don't ever have to work again if I don't want to."

He leans forward. "That's incredible. I had no idea that there was so much money at stake."

"There is if you win. Because I've had sponsorships, and I've done commercials and other things, too. I was smart about it."

"That's sexy."

"The money?"

"The brains," he replies with a laugh. "I don't give a shit about the money."

"That's sexy."

He winks at me. "If you want to do it, you should go. I'll be here when you're done."

I reach over and grab his hand. "I guess I could try it. Come out of retirement for one last hurrah."

"It could be fun."

"I think I have to leave tomorrow."

"Wait, *tomorrow*?"

"I have to be in Moab by Monday, and I want to take the van."

"Wow, that is fast."

"The faster I go, the faster I'm back."

"I like that logic."

"I don't know if I want to go." I turn into Seth's warm body and ignore the fact that the alarm will go off any minute. "It's too damn early."

"Are you going all the way today?"

"No." I kiss his chest. "I'm going to stop in Pocatello, Idaho for the night then go the rest of the way tomorrow."

"Good plan."

The alarm fills the air, and I turn on my back and moan. Cap has been staying with us here at the house, and he stretches on the bed, pushing me against Seth.

"Oh, you're a good boy, aren't you? Are you going to miss me?" I wrap my arms around the big pile of floof and kiss his cheek. "I love you so much. You're the bestest boy ever."

"This could be the first time in my life that I'm jealous of my dog." I laugh over my shoulder at him. "But, like you said last night, the faster you go, the faster you're back. I'll save your spot for you."

"Thanks. Cap will probably hog the bed while I'm gone."

"Probably. Come on, you get in the shower, and I'll make you coffee. Maybe a little bite for the road."

"Don't you have work to see to this morning?"

"Louie knows I'll be late this morning. And he knows why. It's okay."

He kisses me softly, and before I can tug him back to bed, he pulls away.

"Get in the shower," he directs, pointing at me before leaving the room.

I know I'm dragging my feet, but once I'm on the

road, I'll be glad I'm going. It'll be fun to see people I haven't been with in a long time. And the challenges will be fun, too. I'll need a hot tub and a massage when it's over, but I'll kick some ass, just like the old days.

With that pep talk finished, I take a shower and finish packing my suitcase, then pull it behind me to the kitchen, where Seth's made not just coffee but eggs and bacon, as well.

"You spoil me."

"You need to eat," he says and offers his lips as I sidle up beside him. "Do you want some toast, too?"

"No, I need to back off on the carbs for the rest of the week. Thanks, though." I sip my coffee. "What do you have on deck this week while I'm gone?"

"It might snow a little, so we're going to work on getting the last of the cattle out of the mountains and down into the pastures. We need to check on the fences, and Halloween is in a couple of days, so I always volunteer at the fire hall."

"Are there a lot of fires on Halloween?"

"No, there's a big party for the kids there."

I frown into my coffee. I'm going to miss it.

"Here's your breakfast."

"Oh, thanks." Seth makes the *best* bacon in the world. "When I get back, I'm going to start baking. I like to bake this time of year."

"Will there be pumpkin bread?"

I grin and take a bite of my eggs, slipping some down for Cap. "If you want some, yes."

"And shortbread cookies?"

"That's usually for Christmas, but sure."

He stares at me and then pulls me in and kisses me, not caring at all that I have a mouth full of eggs.

"I had no idea that cookies would get this kind of reaction out of you."

"You bake," he says. "I like it."

"So I see." I check the time. "I'll bake all the time if I get this response. Okay, I should go if I want to get to my first stop before dark."

Seth walks me out, helps me load the van, and makes sure that everything is ready for the road. After a long hug and a hot kiss—and lots of ear scratches for Cap—I'm off.

I watch the two of them in my mirror. The tall, strong man that means more to me than anything, and his loyal dog, who's never far from his side. I watch them until I round the bend and they disappear from sight.

I already miss them.

THERE'S NOT MUCH GOING on in Idaho tonight. The drive was pretty, with all of the changing leaves and mountains, but it was lonely.

I used to love being alone in the van, traveling from place to place. Now, it's just...quiet.

Being alone isn't what I want anymore. I like my

van, but it's way more fun when Seth's with me. Maybe he'd like to take a little trip with me sometime when the ranch slows down a bit and he can get away.

Or, maybe I'll end up selling it and buy something more practical for everyday use instead. If I stay in Cunningham Falls, that is.

"Why wouldn't I stay there?" I ask aloud as I secure the van for the night and then hop back inside to have a snack. I *love* it there. I love the people there, and not just Seth's family, but all of those I've met. Annie's my best friend. My regulars that come into the deli are awesome.

Cunningham Falls has become my home.

All day, while I drove away from there, the old feelings of anxiety and dread set up residence in my belly, and I was full of the same insecurities and unhappiness that I've had for so long. It was how I felt when I drove *into* town almost two months ago, but since I've lived there, and since I've been with Seth and working at Little Deli, I haven't had that dread tickling me in the back of the throat.

But it's back now.

And if that doesn't tell me that being in Montana with Seth is where I'm supposed to be, I don't know what does. If I'm at peace there, it's my home.

I glance down as my phone rings.

"Hello?"

"Happy birthday, Remi."

"Mom?" I check the screen. "I didn't recognize the number."

"Oh, I got a new phone last month."

Last month. If I'd needed her over the past month, I would have had no way to reach her. It's shouldn't surprise me. It shouldn't *hurt* me. But it does. It always does.

"Anyway, I called to say happy birthday."

"Thanks. It was yesterday."

"Oh. Well, better late than never."

"Right."

"Oh, I have to run. We're packing for a cruise, and Brittany can't find her Mickey ears from the last one we went on."

"Have a good night."

I hang up and stare out the window.

She still got my birthday wrong, even after our call last month.

She has apparently gone on more than one cruise with the mouse. I didn't know they'd ever been on one before.

I'm not a part of my mother's family.

But I belong in Cunningham Falls. I don't want to go to Moab to compete on a stupid show. I retired for a reason, and it's silly that I let Roberta talk me into doing it. I'm done with that, with doing what I don't want to do, just because I feel obligated.

I want to be where I feel good about myself. Where I fit in.

I hop out of the van and undo all of the nighttime stabilizing I just did, then get back in and start the engine. I dial Roberta's number as I pull back onto the highway, headed toward home.

"Hi, kid, what's up?"

"Get me off that damn show, Bert. I'm not going."

She sighs on the other end. "Are you sure?"

"I'm sure. I'm retired, Bert. I love you, and I'm grateful to you, but it's not what I want anymore."

"Okay, okay. I hear you loud and clear. You take care of yourself, Remi, okay?"

"You, too, Bert. Thank you for everything."

I'm going home.

CHAPTER 16

~SETH~

*I*t's still dark, way too early for the kids to be awake, but I can't sleep, and I'll bet just about anything that my mom's already in the kitchen, making breakfast and getting her day going.

I'm not disappointed when I park my truck by the back door and see the kitchen light on.

I knock softly and then step inside. Mom looks over in surprise, then offers me a smile.

"Don't you ever lock this door?" I ask and lean in to kiss her cheek. "Someone could just walk right in."

"I already went out this morning to gather eggs and feed the chickens," she says as Cap hurries over to get some good morning rubs from her. "What are you two up to?"

"I couldn't sleep," I reply and sit on a stool at the breakfast bar. "Figured I'd come over and see what you're about to put in the oven."

"Scones," she says. "And your grandma and I made fresh apple jam over the weekend, so you can have some of that if you want."

"That sounds pretty damn good. It's handy having a place so close to you. I can bum food."

"That *is* convenient," she agrees and checks on the scones in the oven. "Are you missing Remi?"

"She just left yesterday," I reply, but then nod when she just stares at me. "Yeah. I miss her. But she'll be home this weekend."

"Do you have long-term plans with her, or is this a fun-for-now situation?"

"Mom."

"What? You think I didn't ever have a fun-for-now situation?"

"I really don't want to consider that, to be honest. That's just disgusting."

She narrows her eyes, but she's grinning. Mom likes to tease me.

"I'm gonna marry her."

The smile slips away, and tears fill her eyes. "You didn't tell us you were engaged."

"We're not. Yet. But I know that she's it for me. I can't imagine not being with her, you know? She's been gone for less than twenty-four hours, and I'm lonesome for her. It's the weirdest thing."

"It's love," she replies and sniffles, then wipes away a tear. "And I'm just so happy for you. She's a great girl, and I can see that she is the balance of you. She's adventurous, and you've always had your feet on the ground. I see the way you look at each other. I like to think I still have that with your father."

"You two are ridiculous," I reply and get the smile I was aiming for. "I always thought I'd be a bachelor. I enjoy women, but no one has ever been essential to my well-being. Which sounds dramatic, but—"

"No, it's not dramatic. It's the truth."

"She's important. She's the best part of everything. So, yeah, I'll eventually propose, but there's a lot of time for that."

"Oh, absolutely. Plenty of time. You've only been seeing each other for what? Less than a couple of months?" She pours us each a cup of coffee, then pulls the scones out of the oven.

"Yeah, about that. Gimme the scones and no one gets hurt."

"They have to cool for a minute." She sets out butter and the fresh jam and then settles in across from me, her coffee in her hands. "What else is new?"

"I have a question."

She cocks a brow. "Okay."

"Is it normal for a girl not to tell her boyfriend when her birthday is?"

Mom blinks, clearly thinking it over. "I don't know. I don't think so. What happened?"

"It was her birthday on Friday, and she didn't tell me. Annie texted me and mentioned it, and then I had to scramble. I didn't have time to get her anything, but

I took her out for dinner. I was just kind of pissed that she didn't tell me."

"I guess it could be awkward to work a birthday into conversation."

"Why? Just say, 'So, when's your birthday?'"

"Why didn't *you* ask her? Why is it up to her to bring it up?"

"I—it's not. I didn't think of it."

"We should have a family dinner for her birthday," Mom suggests. "Next weekend, after she gets back."

I reach for a scone and crack it open, spread copious amounts of butter on it, and shove it into my mouth.

"You're such a gentleman," Mom says with complete sarcasm.

"I know," I say around the food. "Good."

I spread jam over the butter on the other half.

"I'll be back later to help Dad and Louie with some stuff in the barn. We need to repair a couple of the stalls after that stallion kicked the hell out of them a few weeks ago."

"No work today?"

"Later," I confirm. "I have to go up and clean some trails, make sure people are staying where they're supposed to. And there's a pair of eagles that I've been watching. They're mated and have built a nest."

"That's exciting," she says. "Be careful up there. I hate that you don't have cell service at work."

"I like it quiet." I shrug and take one more scone for the road. "Is Cap okay with you?"

I break off a piece of my scone and give it to the dog, who wags his tail with enthusiasm.

"Of course. Oh, and will you please give me Remi's number? I'd like to invite her out to lunch."

"Sure." I text her the number and then kiss her on the cheek. "I have to run. I'm meeting Gage for breakfast."

"You just had breakfast."

I just smile at her and head out.

I always feel better after chatting with my mom.

"JESUS IT'S EARLY," Gage mutters as he slides into the booth across from me and gratefully accepts a mug of coffee from the waitress at Ed's.

"Dude, you were in the Army. You're used to getting up at the ass crack of dawn."

His smile is slow. "Not after the night I just had."

"So, things are going well with Tate, then?"

"You could say that." He clinks his mug to mine. "Cheers."

"How're your sister and Sam doing?"

"It's been a hell of a year," Gage says, shaking his head. Sam's sister, Monica, and her husband were killed last year, leaving two kids behind. Sam and Tash took custody of the kids and fell in love in the process.

"But they're figuring it all out. Married life agrees with them. And the kids are doing much better."

"Hard to believe it's been more than a year," I reply softly.

"Life moves on," Gage agrees. "What's up with you? Why are we here so fucking early?"

"Because I have to work today. Remi's out of town, so I thought we could catch up."

I fill him in on Remi's opportunity in Moab.

"She's kind of badass, man," he says when our breakfasts are delivered. "I've seen snippets of her challenges on TV. She's *strong*."

"She's totally badass." I nod, proud of her. "You should have seen her up in the park when she was stuck in that storm. I wanted to throttle her, but also, she held her own. If I hadn't gone up to check on her, it could have ended badly, but only because she's not familiar with the area. When I showed her the way to the shelter, she kept up with me, and she didn't just huddle in a corner once we got inside. She busted ass to help me with the fire and all of the blankets and stuff. She's no coward."

"Strong women are hot," he replies. "I can't tell you how many times I thought for sure Tate would just throw in the towel and tell me to go fuck myself. I would if it was me. But she never has. She grits her teeth and gets the job done. Even when I know for sure she's in pain."

"Is she starting to feel better?"

"Yes, she's making huge gains now. In the beginning, we celebrated the small things, like when she could just lift her left foot off the ground. Or feed herself with her left hand. Now, she barely has a limp. She uses the cane for balance, but I have a hunch she won't even need that by the end of the year."

"That's amazing. You both worked your asses off."

"She did all the work, I just badgered her into it."

"And yet, she lets you see her naked. I'd tell you to go jump off a bridge."

He laughs and then glances toward the door, raising an eyebrow. "Uh, Seth?"

"Yeah?" I follow his gaze and frown when I see Remi walk in. She makes her way to the counter and sits on a stool. "What the hell? Rem?"

She looks around, and then her eyes light up when she sees us. She hurries over and slips into the booth next to me, frames my face in her hands, and plants a kiss on me.

"What the hell are you doing here?"

"It's so early, I didn't want to come out to the ranch in case you were sleeping in. I came back."

"I see that. Why?"

"What can I getcha?" Shirley asks Remi.

"Coffee and corn beef hash, please."

"You got it."

Shirley walks away, and I stare at the love of my life, who just materialized as if I wished her into existence.

"I made it to Pocatello last night," she says and sips

my coffee. "And once I was there, I started to think it all over. Decided I didn't really want to go do this stupid challenge. I only agreed to it because I felt obligated, and that's not a good reason. I missed you, and *this* is where I want to be right now. So, I called my agent and told her to get me out of it, and then I turned around and came home."

"They won't fine you or anything?"

"No." She shakes her head and thanks Shirley when her food comes out so quickly. "I'm sure they're not pleased, but they only gave me a few days' notice. They'll be fine. What did I miss? What are you guys doing?"

"He dragged me out of bed before the sun came up because he was lonely," Gage says, pointing at me. "So, I took pity on him."

"Aw, that's so sweet," Remi says with a satisfied smile and chews on her breakfast.

All I can do is stare at her. She's here. I was up all night, thinking about how much I wished she was next to me, wanting to hold her, talk to her, make love to her.

And here she is.

Because she wants to be here, too.

"Aren't you going to eat that?"

"Yeah." I take a bite of bacon. "So, I guess Annie won't be strapped for help this week, after all."

"Nope." She's damn happy with herself. "I wish I didn't have to work today so I could scoop her up and take her home. Strip her bare and worship every inch of her.

But there will be plenty of time later.

"Didn't you eat at all on the road?" Remi is inhaling her food as if she hasn't eaten in weeks.

"Not really," she says. "I stopped for gas, grabbed a banana somewhere in Idaho. I just wanted to get home, you know?"

Home.

She wanted to get home.

Gage's gaze meets mine, and he raises a brow. I just smile back at him and wrap my arm around my girl.

"I get it," I reply. "And I'm glad you're home. You should have told me you were going out of obligation. I wouldn't have suggested you leave."

"I thought I wanted to." She shrugs and pushes her empty plate away. "But then, I didn't. So, here I am."

"Did you run into any bad weather?" Gage asks. "We could get snow this week."

"I didn't run into much," she replies. "A little rain, but nothing serious. It would suck if the kids had to trick-or-treat in the snow."

"We did it plenty," Gage says with a laugh. "And other years, it was bone dry. You just never know around here."

"Don't go hiking," Remi advises. "Crazy shit happens up in these mountains."

"Anyone could have told you that," Gage says.

"*I* told her that before she went," I say. "But no, she doesn't listen."

"It was September." She holds her hands up in exasperation. "Who gets snow in *September*?"

"Montana does," Gage and I say in unison, making us all laugh.

Remi's phone rings, and she frowns at the display.

"I don't know this number. Hello? Oh, hi, Jillian." Her violet eyes fly to mine. "No, I'm awake. Yeah. I'm actually at Ed's with Seth and Gage. I know, I came home early."

Gage and I share another look as Remi makes lunch arrangements with my mom. And I'm having a silent conversation with Gage.

"She's making plans with your mom."

"So?"

"How serious is this?"

"Pretty damn serious."

"I guess I'm having lunch with your mom tomorrow," Remi says after she hangs up the phone. "With Cara and Lauren, too."

"Nice," Gage says. "I'll have to introduce you to my sister, Natasha, sometime. You'd like her."

"I'm up for that."

"You might meet her at the fire hall on Halloween," I add. "I'm sure she'll bring the kids there."

"I get to go," Remi says with excitement. "I'm happy to help out. This will be fun. I'm *so* glad I came back. Are you going to dress up?"

199

"As a park ranger," I reply and tuck some hair behind her ear. "The kids think I'm cool in my uniform."

"That's not original," she says. "We could go as a couple! Like, Han Solo and Princess Leia or something."

"I look horrible with buns over my ears." I laugh when she narrows her eyes on me.

"As entertaining as this is," Gage says as he tosses some cash on the table, "I have to run. I'm glad you got home safe, Remi."

"Thanks. Sorry to crash your guy time."

"You're much prettier to look at," Gage assures her with a wink, then scoots out of the booth.

"I should get back to the ranch for a bit to help with some things in the barn, and then I have to go to work."

"I thought I'd walk over to see Annie this morning," Remi says. "And then I'm going back to your place to crash. I haven't slept since I left yesterday."

"Don't ever do that again." I urge her chin up with my finger. "That's not safe. I mean it."

"Yes, sir." Her plump lips twitch into a smile. "I won't do it again."

"I'll see you later."

CHAPTER 17

~REMI~

The bell rings over the door when I walk inside of Little Deli. This is my typical day off, but sometimes I stop in just to say hi or grab a coffee.

Or just to chitchat with Annie. She and I have grown really close since I started working for her. She's almost like a big sister now.

"What does a girl need to do to get service around here?" I ask loudly, and then grin when Annie comes out from the kitchen. "Surprise!"

"What in the world are you doing here? Aren't you supposed to be at the Grand Canyon or something by now?"

"Moab," I confirm. "And I decided I didn't want to go."

I tell her all about the adventures of the last twenty-four hours, and when I'm done, she has a huge smile on her pretty face and nods.

"Cunningham Falls has soaked into your blood."

"Something like that. I don't have any need to go back to my old life, Annie. I have a great one here."

"Yes, you do. Well, welcome home. I can tell my husband he's off the hook for helping me out this week."

"He was going to help?"

"Yeah, he took time off work and everything. But now he won't have to do that."

"Jesus, Annie, there was no need for that. You should have said something."

"No way. I'm just grateful that I have you. I can always work around a little time off here and there. Don't worry about it. Honest."

"*You* need a day off, you know."

"That's why I close on Mondays. What are you going to do now that you're home this week?"

"I'm going to nap the rest of today. I'll wing what comes next."

"Enjoy your nap! Take an extra thirty for me, okay?"

"I got you." I wink and then wave as I walk out the door and head back down the street to my van.

The air is crisp and clean. The mountains are just gorgeous with little wisps of clouds barely covering the peaks. I wave at Ty, who regularly comes into the deli, as he jogs by, his shirt soaked through with sweat.

It's a quiet Sunday morning in this little town tucked in the mountains.

Yes, it's good to be home.

SOMETHING ISN'T RIGHT.

I've been back at Seth's for an hour. I took a shower, put on some comfy clothes, and threw a load of laundry into the machine, then my stomach started to cramp horribly.

It feels like something inside is fighting to get out.

Like an alien.

"Oh, shit." I cover my mouth with my hand and run for the bathroom. I heave until there's surely nothing left in me. And then, when I finally manage to wipe off my face with a nearby towel, I have to hurry and sit on the toilet.

Jesus, what's happening?

The next thirty minutes are a blur. So much pain, and so many horrible things coming out of my body.

"I'm dying." I lie on the cool tile and stare at the ceiling. "This is how it ends."

And then I have to throw up again.

I try to call Seth, but he's probably already up in the park and has no cell service. Sure enough, I go straight to voicemail.

I don't know what to do. Something tells me I shouldn't be alone.

So, I call Jillian.

"Hey, Remi, how's it going?"

"I'm not okay," I choke out and fight back a panic attack. "Something's wrong, and I don't know what to do."

"Seth said you're back in town. Are you at his house?"

"Yes. Oh, God, I can't stop throwing up."

"Hang tight, honey. Cara and I will be right there."

I let the phone fall to the floor and hug the toilet. If I move away, I'm afraid I'll have to throw up again and won't make it back in time.

More heaving.

More cramps.

Absolute agony.

"Remi?"

"In the bathroom." I try to yell out, but it's a whisper.

"Oh, honey." There's commotion around me. The faucet runs, someone pulls my hair back into a ponytail and rubs my back.

"Can't stop throwing up. And I had diarrhea. And, oh my God, my stomach."

"Okay, it's going to be okay." Jillian wipes my face with the cool cloth, and it feels like Heaven.

"Oh, God." I lean over and keep throwing up.

"I'm going to call Josh and tell him to bring some supplies," Cara says behind me. Jillian keeps rubbing my back and presses the cool cloth against my neck.

"It's okay."

"Not okay." I lean my forehead on the toilet seat and feel like crying. "What are you doing?"

"I'm soothing you. Doesn't your mother do this for you when you're sick?"

"No."

I throw up some more, and then I feel too weak to do anything else. Jillian helps me to the bedroom, where Cara's already turned down the bed.

"Josh will be here in ten minutes with some electrolytes and crackers," she informs us as I fall onto the bed. "I hate to be the one to ask this, but Remi, could you be pregnant?"

"Pregnancy doesn't cause diarrhea," Jillian hisses.

"I don't think so. Unlikely." I take a deep breath and will my stomach to settle just as my phone rings. I frown at Annie's name and answer on speaker.

"'llo?"

"Tell me you didn't eat the corned beef hash this morning at Ed's," she says. "It was bad. I guess a bunch of people are sick from it."

"Sure did." I swallow hard. "So sick."

"Oh, man. I'm so sorry, Remi. Do you need anything?"

"Hi, Annie, this is Jillian. Cara and I are here, but we'll be sure to let you know if anything comes up."

"You do that. Get some rest, Rem. I'll call you later and check in."

"Thanks."

I click off and moan. I don't think I've ever been so sick in my life. "You guys don't have to stay. I think the worst is over. I hope."

"We're staying," Cara insists. "At least until Seth comes home. Do you think you can take a tiny sip of water?"

"Nothing." I wrinkle my nose.

"Okay. It's okay," Cara croons.

They're hovering. They're worried. I can see it on their faces.

"If you get too dehydrated, you'll have to go to the hospital," Jillian says.

"This just started. Let me settle down, and then I'll try the water."

"That's fair," Cara says and then runs out of the room when we hear a knock on the door.

"That's probably Josh with the supplies," Jillian says with a smile. "You've already gotten rid of most of what you ate. You should start to feel better."

"I got rid of everything I've eaten since I was nine," I reply and then turn into the fetal position as more cramps rack my body. "It's like someone is squeezing my stomach in a vise."

"I'm so sorry," Jillian whispers and wipes another cloth on my face. It feels cool and nice.

And weird.

"You don't have to do that."

"Oh, I'm sorry if it doesn't feel good."

I sigh when the cramp passes. "That's not it. I'm just not used to being taken care of, that's all."

Jillian is quiet for a moment. "I hate that your mom didn't take care of you when you were sick."

"Yeah, well, she's not a stellar mom."

"Not all mothers are born with the nurturing gene," she says softly and tentatively wipes the rag over my cheek. "Cara and I are mothers, honey. And we're here to take care of you. You can't do it yourself right now. But if you're uncomfortable, just say so, and I'll back off, okay?"

My eyes want to fill with tears, so I blink rapidly. "Thanks. Really, thank you for coming so fast. I was scared."

"I know. I know you were."

"I have supplies," Cara says softly. "And Josh is trying to get in touch with Seth. He'd be upset if he knew you were so sick and no one could reach him."

"I feel like I'm a huge pain in the ass." I swallow hard, willing my body not to make me throw up again.

"This is what family does," Cara says, so matter-of-factly that my eyes fill with tears once more. "Don't worry, sweetheart. We'll get you feeling like yourself in no time. I promise."

"Oh, God."

I have to run for the bathroom again for round two. It's not as bad as the first round, but when I'm done, sweat covers me.

"Who knew food could be so angry?" I ask as Jillian

starts the shower for me. I don't even feel self-conscious as I strip down and step into the warm water. It's not too hot, just enough that it doesn't make me shiver.

"My hips remind me just how angry food can be, every time I eat cupcakes," Cara says with a wink.

I take in her curly blonde hair, her curvy body, and grin. "You're completely adorable. I can see why Josh fell hard for you. And Seth, now that I think of it."

"Seth fell for me?" Cara asks in confusion.

"He told me that you were his safe person for a long time," I reply and turn the water off, then take the towel Cara offers. "And I can see why. You're wonderful. You're both just wonderful."

"I think I have something in my eye," Jillian says, wiping at her face.

"Me, too," Cara agrees and sniffles. "And now I know why he loves *you* so much, Remi. Damn it. I'm getting all sentimental."

I step into the clean pajamas that Jillian brought in, and once I'm all clothed, Jillian pulls us in for a group hug.

"I know I feel gross, but thank you both so much for helping me. Now I have to fall back into the bed."

They laugh and wipe at tears, then help me back to the bed. Jillian actually tucks me in and kisses my forehead, and when another cramp moves through my belly, and I moan in pain, they're there to talk me through it.

God, it feels like I'm going to die.

I manage to fall asleep. I can hear people speaking softly around me, but I'm so weak, so exhausted, I drift. The cloth is on my head, and then it's gone.

I toss and turn.

And then I have to run for the bathroom again.

Finally, what seems like an eternity later, I hear Seth.

"What's wrong with her? What's going on?"

"Food poisoning," I hear Jillian say. They whisper. And then he's with me, wrapping his arms around me and pulling me against him. He kisses my forehead.

"Oh, baby. I'm so sorry."

"Sucks," I mutter with my eyes closed. "So tired."

"Just sleep. And then we'll get some broth in you."

The mention of food makes my stomach roil. But lying here with him feels so good.

"If you need me, just call," Jillian says, and I open my eyes.

"Thank you." I reach for her hand, and she lets me take it. "Thank you for saving me. I was scared."

"You gave *us* a scare, too. But you'll be okay, and Seth's here with you. I'm just down the road."

"Thank you," I say again and fall asleep against Seth's chest.

~

I'M WRAPPED IN A BLANKET, sitting on the front porch swing. It's past midnight. I feel like I went four rounds with the champ.

I needed some fresh air, so I tiptoed out of the bedroom, grabbed a blanket, and came outside. Seth was sleeping soundly, and I didn't want to wake him up. I kept thinking about Jillian and Cara and everything they did for me today.

They cared for me.

And while my mother has never been mean, she was never a maternal person, at least with me. She was with my younger siblings, and it always confused me.

But now that I'm in a loving relationship and have spent a good amount of time with Seth's family, I think I get it.

I was a daily reminder of the man that she couldn't stand. I was with her because of duty. But I wasn't part of her ideal family. And, damn it, that's not my fault.

Seth's experience, once his dad married Jillian, could have been the same. But it was exactly the opposite. Jillian loves him as if he came from her body. His family is affectionate and loving, and no one is left out. No one is ever made to feel like they're less than.

My mother's lack of a decent-parent gene isn't my fault at all. And I think it's time that I let that go. It could stay with me, make me angry, frustrate me. Or I can just accept that she is who she is and move forward. If she's missing from my life, that's on her. Not me.

It took coming to Montana and meeting some incredible people to make me realize that.

"Here you are." Seth shuffles out onto the porch and joins me on the swing. "I got worried when I couldn't find you."

"I'm sorry. I thought you'd sleep through it."

"How are you doing?"

"A little better. I'm not throwing up anymore, so I consider that a win. I just feel weak and tired."

"I'm so sorry that you got sick, baby." He wraps me tightly in his arms and sets the swing into motion. The stars tonight are insanely bright, and an owl hoots in the distance.

"I'll never eat corned beef hash again in my life."

He chuckles and kisses the top of my head. "I don't blame you there. I don't think I will either, in support."

He's quiet for a moment, and then he says, "You probably shouldn't go to the Halloween party tomorrow, you know."

I scowl up at him. "Damn it, Seth, that's just mean. I really wanted to go."

"I know." He kisses my cheek. "But you need to rest, babe. You were *so* sick."

I pout. "It's not fair."

"I'll stay home with you."

I shake my head. "No. You're volunteering. You should go."

"No way. If you don't go, I don't go."

He kisses my head.

211

I bury my face in his shoulder and breathe him in. He smells like the soap in the shower and like...*Seth.*

It's the best.

"We should probably go back to bed," he finally says.

"Yeah. But let's sit here in the quiet, just for a few more minutes."

He leans back and looks down at me. "You sure you're okay?"

"I am. I was just thinking. Coming to terms with some things."

"Anything you need to talk about?"

"No." I stand and offer him my hand. "No, I have it figured out for now."

CHAPTER 18

I like having her here. All of her. At this point, after spending more than a month in the house, she's pretty much unpacked her van, and all of her things are mingled with mine.

She has closet space. Drawers in the dresser. She bought fancy little autumn towels for the kitchen that I'm not allowed to use to dry my hands because they're *decorative.*

Without a declaration from one of us, she's moved in. And I love that it was completely organic. She just *lives here.* Like it's as natural as breathing.

Her slippers are by the couch where she toed them off last night when we watched the finale of the show she was supposed to be on.

I cleaned her hair out of the shower drain this morning.

And I don't care at all. Because I *love* having her

here.

"Ugh." She sits on the side of the bed and presses a hand to her stomach as I walk into the bedroom.

"What's wrong?"

"I just threw up again. I didn't think that food poisoning lasted a week."

"It doesn't." I prop my hands on my hips and frown in concern. "You really should see a doctor, babe."

"It's probably just the flu."

I shake my head. "I don't think so. I'm not sick. If you've had the flu for a week, odds are good that I would have caught it, too."

"Right." She furrows her brow and looks up at the ceiling. "Shit. If they jinxed me, I'm going to punch them in the face. Well, just Cara. She brought it up."

"Why are you going to punch Cara in the face? And just to warn you, I love you, but I can't have you punching my aunt Cara, babe."

"When she and Jillian were here last week when the sickness hit, she asked if I could be pregnant. But, of course, that wasn't it. Because I ate the corned beef that made others sick, and we're always careful. But—"

"But?"

"But food poisoning doesn't last a week, Seth."

I blink at her. "Maybe it *is* the flu."

Everything in me shuts down. I don't want to think about the alternative.

"I'm sure it's nothing," she repeats and pastes a smile on her face. "Maybe I ate something else that didn't agree with me. Or it was watching that jerk, Derek, on the show finale last night. That dude should *not* have won."

"He looks smarmy," I reply and try to push the idea of a pregnancy from my mind.

"You should see him in person." She gives a pretend shiver. "Are you off to the barn for the day?"

"Yeah, we'll be out riding fence until lunchtime, but I'll have my cell if you need me."

"Okay." She wraps her arms around my shoulders. "We're okay, right?"

"Of course. Yeah, we're great. Feel better, babe."

"Have a good day."

I kiss her lightly, grab my hat, and hurry out to my truck. I've never wanted to get to the barn so badly in my life.

My stomach is in knots, and it has nothing to do with an illness. I'm cold. And damn it, I'm just...panicked.

I park behind the barn and hurry inside. Dad and Josh are talking with Louie when I approach.

"There you are, kid," Louie says, but his face sobers when he sees me. "I think I'll go check on that foal."

He walks away, and I'm left under the scrutiny of Josh and Dad.

"What?"

"What's wrong with you?" Josh asks.

"Nothing. Let's go ride fence. Wait, is there a new foal?"

"Bullshit," Dad says quietly, and both of them cross their arms over their chests and stare me down like they used to when I was in trouble as a kid. "Talk."

I scratch my chin and shake my head. "No."

Dad narrows his eyes. "If you won't talk about it, I can't use you today. I need your head in the game. So you can go."

"I think she's pregnant."

The words are out of my mouth before I can reel them back in again, and the two men I respect the most in the world just stare at me.

"She's still sick," I continue and tell them about our conversation this morning. "Food poisoning doesn't last a week. We all know that."

They share a look and then turn their gazes back on me.

"And you're not happy about it," Dad guesses.

"I'm not dad material." My voice is flat, devoid of any of the emotion I have roiling inside of me. "I had no plans to ever have kids. Get married? Sure. I can do that. But being a parent isn't in my future."

"So, what are you saying? If she's pregnant, you'll… what?" Josh asks. "Turn her away? Cast her aside?"

The very thought fills me with rage and despair. But the idea of a baby? It paralyzes me in fear.

"I don't know. I don't fucking know." I pace away and take off my hat, scratching my head before slamming it back on again. "Everyone knows, especially me, that I can *not* have kids."

"Why?" Dad demands as he tilts his head and narrows his eyes. "Why can't you be a father?"

I chew on my lip. How do I say this without hurting his feelings?

"Did your mom and I fuck you up?" he continues.

"Not you and Jillian," I reply and then swear under my breath, pacing back and forth. "You guys are the best. All of you. And the kids are all well-adjusted people."

"But not you?" Josh asks.

"I'm way better than I was the day that bitch dropped me off on this ranch." I shake my head. "But damn it, *her* gene pool is in me. And I'd give just about anything to make that not true. For Jillian to be my biological mom. But she's not. And I'll be goddamned if I'll pass on anything Kensie gave me to a baby. That's just not fair."

"Seth—" Dad begins, but I cut him off.

"No, it's not just that. Look, you know that Kensie was a shitty mom and that I had it pretty bad before I came here. I don't want to tell you all of the things that happened, but let me just say that I've seen too much, and I have too much bad in me to be a dad."

"Whoa," Dad says and puts his hands up, palms out. "Stop right there. What in the *hell* are you talking about?"

I shake my head. "Nevermind. I shouldn't have brought it up. I'm just a mess. And you're probably right. I shouldn't be here today."

"What did you see, Seth?"

"Nothing. It's nothing."

"It's not nothing, goddamn it," Dad counters. "We can't help you if we don't know what's going on."

"It was a long time ago, and it's over, so it doesn't matter."

"It's clearly not over for you," Josh replies. "And if this isn't your safe place, then I don't know what is, Seth. We love you, and nothing's ever going to change that, so you need to talk to us. Tell us what in the hell has you so twisted up inside."

Jesus, I don't want to do this. But I need advice. I need to talk to them because with the way I feel right now, if Remi's pregnant, I don't know what I'll do.

So, I talk. I talk more than I ever have before, and I tell them everything. I don't leave anything out. When I'm done and look up at them, my uncle Josh has tears in his eyes, and my dad looks like he wants to kill someone with his bare hands.

I'm pretty sure he has done that in the past.

"How do I bring all of that to a kid?" I ask at last. "It's not fair. It's too much."

"So, what you're saying is, because the woman who birthed you was a piece of shit who allowed other pieces of shit to treat you like a dumpster when you weren't old enough to fend for yourself, you're not worthy of having a family?" Josh asks. "You're not good enough to raise a child in a loving and respectful house? You grew up in a family that's exactly that:

loving and respectful. Hell, you practically raised your younger siblings and cousins. You're their favorite person in the world."

"That's different," I whisper.

"No," Dad says at last. "It's not different. It shows who you *are*. I need to say this, for the record. If she were still alive, I'd fucking kill her. Slowly. Painfully."

I tighten my jaw and nod once.

"I'd hold her for you," Josh mutters. "After I killed the assholes with her."

"I'm no shrink, but Seth, you're not going to be a shitty dad because those awful things happened to you when you were a kid."

"Hell, no," Josh says. "If anything, it'll make you *more* protective. *More* grateful that you have something so great."

I stop and frown, considering. "I guess I never thought of it like that."

"You and Remi have an incredible built-in support system here on the ranch," Dad reminds me. "With your grandma here, your mom and Cara, and hell, all of the kids, that baby won't go without love and attention. In fact, you'll be kicking us all out of your house. You'll be sick of everyone."

"He doesn't kick me out of his house," Uncle Josh says. "I'm his favorite."

"I don't know, it scares me."

"It should terrify you," Dad says with a nod. "Being a dad is the hardest thing you'll ever do."

"Says the man with a dozen kids," I reply.

"Four. Four kids. And I don't regret a minute of it. Well," he amends, shaking his head, "I regret how I handled things when you were young—now more than ever."

"It wasn't your fault," I remind him.

"Yeah, it was. And I'm sorry, son. I'm so fucking sorry."

"I'm fine now."

"So fine that you think you can't have babies," he counters. "Hell, Seth, we all have baggage. I couldn't listen to loud noises for *years* after I got home. Still don't like them. I was married to a woman who systematically tried to ruin my life, hurt my kid. And when I got here, you were so angry, you refused to be in the same room with me, and I was scared of my own shadow. But with time and love, we figured it out."

"I'll never forget that Fourth of July," I say softly as the memory forms perfectly in my mind. "That first Fourth of July at the beach celebration, when you thought the fireworks were gunfire and covered me, trying to save me. I realized how much you loved me and that everything I'd been told before was just a lie."

"Just like what you've told yourself for all these years is a lie," he agrees. "Being damaged doesn't mean you can't heal. That you can't have wonderful things. Like children. Just don't do what I did when I found out that Jillian was pregnant with the twins."

"Oh, definitely don't do that," Josh agrees.

"What did you do?"

Dad sighs and rubs his forehead. "I might have accused her of getting pregnant on purpose and lying to me about being infertile."

I stare at the man I love more than almost anyone. "I want to punch you so hard right now."

"Trust me, she punished me. We've both had a hard time, you and I."

"Wait. When she left us, and you said that sometimes things just don't work out, that was why?"

"Yeah."

"And then Kensie showed up here, and Jillian stood up for me, punched Kensie out, and Jillian still left that day. Because you're stupid?"

"Oh, yeah, I was stupid. *Was* is the operative word there."

"Sometimes, you're still stupid," Josh says philosophically.

"For fuck's sake, I wouldn't accuse Remi of trapping me or something."

"Yeah, don't do that. They really hate that," Dad says and rubs a hand over his chest as if that's where Mom shoved him.

"What did Remi say this morning?" Josh asks. "Does *she* think she's pregnant?"

"She actually didn't sound excited at the thought, either, and then she gave me some fake smiles and said that everything would be okay. Of course, I was an idiot and didn't do much to reassure her. But damn it, I was freaked out."

"It's perfectly okay if you're not ready for kids *today*," Josh says. "You and Remi haven't been together that long, and it came as a surprise. But I hope you reconsider thinking that you can't *ever* have kids, or that you'd be a bad father. Because that couldn't be further from the truth, Seth."

"I agree," Dad says. "You've come a long, long way since you were that scared, angry boy. You're strong, you're good, and the only thing you got from Kensie is that weird cowlick in the front of your hair. There's nothing of her in you."

I take a deep breath. I feel a lot better after talking with them. Maybe I could be a dad.

Just hopefully not yet. Not today. I want time to get used to the idea. To spend with Remi. Hell, I just found her. I want time with her.

"Let's go ride the fence," I suggest. "It'll help clear my head, and I won't be such a jerk when I go home later. I'm glad I talked to you both. I have some thinking to do, but I'm not quite as messed up as I was when I got here."

"You'll be a good dad," Dad says and tugs my hat off so he can ruffle my hair. "The fact that you're worried about being a good parent says a lot."

"And if you screw up, we'll be here to razz you about it," Josh adds. "Maybe you should buy Remi flowers or something. Just to cover your ass."

CHAPTER 19

"Oh, this is bad." I bury my face in my hands and rub my eyes as I hear Seth's truck drive away. I feel like shit. I've been much better since the day I got so sick, but I'm still not one hundred percent. And from the look on Seth's face just now, I'd say he's not okay with the thought of a pregnancy. I've never seen him look so scared, even that day up in a snowstorm in the park.

He ran out of here like the house was on fire.

And why wouldn't he? We both have parent issues, and so much to talk about before we even start to think about having kids. But he'd be a great parent. I know he would.

"Jesus, Rem, you don't even know for sure you're pregnant."

I brush my hair, loop it into a simple bun, and dress

in blue jeans and a sweatshirt. Without even thinking about coffee or breakfast, I take off toward town.

I need two things: a pharmacy and Annie.

I'm in and out of the pharmacy in just five minutes. Easy-peasy. On my way to Annie's, I call and let her know I'm on my way.

She sounds tired, and I hate interrupting her morning, but this is an emergency.

"Hey," she says when she opens the door. "What's up? Why are you in town this early in the morning?"

"I know it's your one day off, and I'm sorry, but I need a friend today."

"No need to be sorry." She ushers me in. "The kids just left for school, and the hubs is at the office, so it's just you and me."

"Good. That's good." I hold the plastic bag I brought with me in the air. "I need your bathroom."

Annie's eyes go round, and she stares at the bag, and then at me. "*Remi.*"

"I know. No, I don't know, actually. Which is why I have four of these tests."

"I hope you have to pee," she says as she leads me down a hall to a bathroom. "Here you go."

"Thanks. This shouldn't take long."

Okay, it takes longer than I thought because I have to read the instructions and figure out how to aim to pee on the stick, but ten minutes later, I open the door.

"Well?"

"I don't want to look," I admit with a sigh. "Seth's not okay with a baby, Annie."

"He *said* that?"

"No, but I saw it in his face this morning. Raging terror and uncertainty. He doesn't *want* kids."

"Well, if you're pregnant, it just is what it is, and you'll figure it out," Annie says. "You love each other."

"We've known each other for six minutes," I whisper and close my eyes, praying fervently that I'm not pregnant. Not now.

"Hey. I knew my husband for five weeks when we got engaged. Sometimes, you just know. Besides, this whole conversation could be for nothing. It might be negative, and you've just got a stomach thing or hormonal shit going on."

"Right." I nod and pray with all my might that that's the case. "Could it be hormonal shit? Either way, I think Seth and I need to have a serious conversation later."

"I think, if you're not pregnant, you need to decide if having a family is important to you. Because if it is, and you know that Seth doesn't want children, that could be a deal-breaker for you two, Remi. You can't expect someone to change their mind just because you love them and you wish it to be true."

"No, I know that. You're right. Okay, here goes nothing."

~

I HAVE the van packed and am ready to go. Seth should be home anytime, and I don't know how this conversation will go. On the one hand, it could be fantastic. On the other, not so much. And I wanted to be prepared to leave just in case. I still have a space reserved at the RV park outside of town, where I spent the first few weeks I lived here.

I've scrubbed the bathroom and kitchen, mopped all the hardwood in the house, and did a ton of laundry. I even changed the sheets on the bed, and I just did that yesterday.

I had to direct my nervous energy somewhere.

Seth's truck comes rumbling up the road, the tires crunching the gravel, and he parks in his usual spot. I walk out onto the porch, and he stops in his tracks, his dark eyes serious as he watches me, searching my face.

"Did you have a lot of fence to mend?" I ask as I sit on the swing and pull my feet up. Seth leans on the railing opposite me, still serious, still searching.

"Not too much. It was a good day to be on a horse. How was your day?"

I nod, looking out at the trees that separate Seth's house from his parents'. "Fine."

We're silent for a moment, and then I look back at him and shake my head.

"No, it wasn't fine. I'm not *fine* at all."

"Talk to me, babe."

Babe. It's the first sign of hope that I've seen from him since this morning.

"I know that the idea of kids isn't high on your list of good things," I begin. "And I've never really thought that I'd have a family, either. It definitely wasn't in my plans or even on my radar."

"You're pregnant," he says.

"I didn't say that." He's not showing any emotion on his face at all. He's not giving anything away, and I hate that I feel so distant from him. I *hate* it. "But I think, at some point, whether I'm pregnant right now or not, I want kids, Seth."

"Did you take a test?"

"Four of them," I confirm. "I spent all morning at Annie's house, drinking water and peeing on sticks."

"And?"

"I'm not pregnant."

"Oh, thank God." He hangs his head in relief, and I just sit here, staring at him.

"I'll be out of your hair in a few minutes." I stand and walk toward the door, but he catches my arm and stops me.

"Wait, what? Where are you going?"

"I'm leaving, Seth. I just told you that I want kids someday, and you were so relieved that I'm *not* pregnant now, that I thought you were going to throw confetti and strike up the freaking band!"

"Were you *hoping* to be pregnant, Rem?"

"No. No, I wasn't. I'm not ready. And I know you're not ready. But I also could have used a little more tenderness from you today. Instead, you ran away, and you're distant, and when I told you that I *do* want kids someday, you said nothing. Your silence speaks volumes."

He's still silent, his gorgeous eyes turbulent as he watches me. And *still*, there's no emotion.

"Say something!" I push him in the chest and knock him back a step. "Say something, you big jerk! Because I'm about to give up on everything we've started. My van is packed. I can be gone in ten minutes."

"I don't want you to leave," he finally says. "I know I've been an ass today, and I do not want you to go. But I'm still working out how I feel about the kids thing. I've spent all day talking it over with my dad and Uncle Josh."

"You *told* them?"

"Fuck, yes, I did. You have Annie, and I have them, Rem. I trust them more than anyone."

"Okay." I nod and take a deep breath, calming myself down. "Okay, I'm sorry about that. You're right."

"They talked some sense into me, and I know that if you had been pregnant right now, we would have made it work. Don't yell at me," he says when I open my mouth. "I know that sounds douchey, but you're *not* pregnant, Rem, and I'm just thinking out loud. I'm being honest."

"Okay," I say again.

"I thought that I would be a shitty parent because of my past. Because of what happened to me when I was a kid. And Dad and Josh put it into perspective for me. I don't necessarily think that anymore. I just don't want a pregnancy to be a surprise. I know that can't always be the case, but if and when you and I decide to start a family, I want to plan a little. Hell, *you're* the planner in this relationship, that should make you happy."

For the first time, hope fills my chest.

"I'm okay with planning," I say softly. "Later."

"Definitely later."

"Not too much later. I don't want to be seventy when they graduate from high school, you know."

His lips twitch. "I haven't even proposed yet."

I have to swallow hard.

"We haven't spent the holidays together or planned *anything*. We're just starting this thing between us, and I don't want to rush, Rem. I want to take my time with you, savor every second of this time because I'm only doing this once. With you. There's no need to rush it."

"No." I step forward, so relieved and so much in love that I can hardly stand it. I wrap my arms around his shoulders and lean in. "There's no need to rush. Just, someday."

"Someday. But I can tell you what's going to happen *today.*"

He picks me up in that effortless way he does and carries me inside. I laugh. "You stink from being on a horse all day. You need a shower."

He grins and carries me through to the bathroom. "You can take one with me."

~

"WAKE UP." Seth kisses my cheek and then my shoulder.

"What time is it?"

"It's about three," he whispers. "And I have something to show you."

"I've seen it. And while it's impressive, I'm tired, Seth. Let a girl sleep."

He chuckles and pulls the covers back, then wraps me in my favorite throw blanket since I'm as naked as the day I was born, before lifting me from the bed.

"I can walk." But I lay my head on his shoulder and sigh deeply as he strolls through the house.

"I like carrying you." He kisses my cheek and opens the front door.

"Holy shit," I whisper. There are candles lit on the railings of the porch, extra blankets on the swing, and a steaming hot pizza on a little table. "Where'd you get that pizza?"

"I can't divulge my secrets," he says as he sets me down and then cuddles up next to me. "The best part is over in the distance."

He passes me a slice of the pie and points to the horizon where green, blue, and purple lights fill the sky.

"Aurora borealis," I whisper in awe as I munch on the pizza and Seth blows out the candles around us so we can see the lights better. "And it snowed?"

"First true snow of the season," he confirms. "I knew you wouldn't want to miss this."

"Did you arrange for it all? Not just the pizza but the lights? The snow?"

"I'm not on those kinds of terms with Mother Nature, but it worked out pretty well, don't you think?"

"It's gorgeous," I confirm. We sit in comfortable silence, eating and watching the show. After one piece, I'm done with the food and curl up into Seth's side. "We get to live here."

He smiles down at me. "Yeah. It's pretty great, isn't it?"

"What did I ever do in my life to deserve this?"

He kisses my head and then tips my chin up so he can take my lips. "I love you so much, sweetheart."

"I love you, too." I move under the blankets and straddle Seth, right on the swing. My hands brace against the white wood behind him, and his hands roam up and down my bare back. The cool air feels amazing on my warm skin.

"I had no idea you were an exhibitionist," he murmurs before I kiss his lips. His thumb flicks one of my nipples, making my core tighten.

"There's no one out here to see us. I think it's kind of sexy to make love out here, in the cold, under the northern lights."

He pulls a condom out of his pocket, and that arrogant smile on his lips flashes. "I like the way you think, babe."

When I lower over him, we both sigh. When he cups my ass and urges me, moves me up and down in long, slow strokes, I moan.

"Jesus, you make me crazy," he growls.

"Same." I pick up the pace. "God, Seth."

"Mine." My eyes find his bright ones. "You're *mine*."

I grin, tipping my forehead to his. "You're mine."

And when we fall over the edge into ecstasy, surrounded by cool air and bright, dancing lights, he pulls me to him and holds me close until we catch our breath.

"Mine," he whispers once more.

CHAPTER 20

~SETH~

"*I* don't get a lot of uninterrupted sleep since I met you," Remi says with a frown as she rolls over in bed. "It's pathetically early. I know it's Christmas, but you have to be past the age of waking up in the middle of the night to see if Santa came."

I grin at her. God, she's the most beautiful woman I've ever seen. Even when she's scowling at me for waking her.

"It's not the middle of the night," I inform her. "It's six. I've been up for an hour."

"Do we have to go to the big house this *early*?"

"We're not going over there yet," I reply and kiss her soft cheek. "Just get dressed. You'll see what's up soon enough."

She sits and stretches her arms up over her head. The covers fall, revealing her stellar breasts.

"Nope, you're not going to distract me with sex."

She grins. "I tried. Okay, fine. I'll be ready in ten."

True to her word, we're soon off in my truck, headed toward the barn. Once inside, I spot Louie ready for us, Magic's reins in his hands.

"What's this?" Remi asks with a frown.

"You'll see," I repeat. "Thanks, Louie. I'm sorry to do this to you on Christmas morning."

"Don't you worry 'bout me. Here's your coffee and a little something your mama sent down for you." He winks at me. "Have fun."

"There's only one horse saddled up," Remi says after Louie has gone.

"We're going together," I inform her and help her into the saddle and then swing on behind her, cuddling her close. "We have coffee, and it looks like Mom made huckleberry muffins."

"Oh, gimme," she says and bites into one as Magic walks us out of the barn. "They're still warm. This is a nice new Christmas tradition. Good thing we bundled up, it's damn cold out here."

I smile and kiss her hair. My girl can talk, and I love it. The sky is just starting to lighten, and we can make out the outline of the mountains in the distance. The timing is going to be absolutely perfect.

When we're less than half a mile from our destination, I start to talk, breaking the stillness.

"I've heard this story for most of my life," I begin. "How my uncle and my dad brought Aunt Cara and Mom out here like this to watch the sunrise. There's a particular spot over here that is just amazing, especially at this time of day."

"It's so still. So quiet," she murmurs. "As if the snow has hushed everything."

It's my favorite time of year—when the world is quiet and chilly.

The snow brightens a bit as the sun starts sending pink and purple into the sky. As we pass the cemetery, I notice a white owl perched on my grandpa's headstone, watching us with round, wise eyes.

Something tells me, deep down, that my grandpa is here, and that he approves of what I have planned this morning.

I urge Magic to stop just about ten yards from the special tree, and we sit in silence as we watch the sun come up over the mountains.

"Wow," Remi says. "Merry Christmas, babe."

I bury my nose in her hair and breathe her in. "Merry Christmas. I have something else to show you."

She turns back to look at me. *"More?"*

"Over here." Magic takes us closer to the tree, and I point to the freshly carved heart with initials inside.

S.K.

R.C.

"Oh, Seth."

"I was happy here, before you." Remi turns on the

horse until she's fully facing me. "I knew that I'd be here forever, working this land, caring for the animals here and up in the park, and I never wanted anything more than that. Before you."

I take her hand and kiss it.

"This ranch, and the people on it, saved me, Remi. It's my safe place. But something was always missing, and I didn't even realize it. Some*one*. You arrived, and it was as though a missing puzzle piece just clicked into place. You are the best part of my life, and I hope that you'll agree to stay here, with me. Make a family here, and help me carry on the legacy that Clifford King started all those years ago. Will you marry me, Remi?"

A tear slips down her sweet cheek, but she doesn't wipe it away. She presses her lips closed, and then she smiles and nods. "Of course, I will. I love it here on the ranch so much. I love your family. But more than any of that, I love *you*. Every bit of you, the dark places, and the funny ones. I'm a better person for knowing you, Seth King."

I kiss her forehead softly, overcome with emotion and love.

And then, I pull back to offer her the ring my grandmother gave me last week.

"This was my great-grandmother's ring," I say, holding it in the golden sunlight on this incredible Christmas morning. "It's a Montana sapphire, and I had a halo of diamonds added to it."

"Holy shit, Seth, this is stunning."

"I hope it fits."

When I slide it on, it's a *perfect* fit.

"Thank you. I'll treasure it always."

"You're welcome." The kiss is slow and lingering, and finally, I adjust Remi back into the saddle so we can ride back to the house to celebrate Christmas with the family.

When we ride past the cemetery, the owl is still there on my grandpa's headstone.

Don't worry, Gramps. I'll take care of everything. I've got this.

The bird of prey hoots and then flies away, gliding in front of us before disappearing into the trees.

"Did you see—?"

"Yeah. I saw him."

"Is everyone up this early?" Remi asks when we walk from the barn to the big house to join the others for Christmas.

"They've been up for a while," I reply with a smile. "I told them not to wait for us for the whole present-opening thing. The kids might revolt."

"Good idea," she says with a laugh and follows me up the back steps of the house. I walk in without knocking.

No one's in the kitchen.

That's unusual, but not unheard of, given that it's Christmas.

"They're probably in the living room." Hand in hand, we walk through to the formal living room where Mom likes to put her Christmas tree, but they're not there, either.

"Seth."

I glance down, and Remi points out the window, where the whole family, including Ty, Lauren, and Layla, are currently engaged in a massive snowball fight.

In their pajamas.

"This is the year for new traditions," I say with a wink, and we hurry outside to join them.

"Insurgents," Dad yells, and everyone turns to us. But Remi and I hold our own. Before long, the entire family has collapsed in the snow in a fit of giggles.

"What in the hell brought this on?" I ask as I lie in the snow and try to catch my breath.

"We had to find something to do until you and Remi arrived," Mom says as she helps Cara to her feet. "So, I declared a snowball fight."

"I creamed her," Troy announces. "It was awesome."

"And you're engaged," Cara says as I stand. She walks to me and cups my face in her hands, her eyes shining with tears. I lean down to kiss her cheek, and she whispers in my ear. "I told you, all those years ago, that you deserve this, my sweet boy."

I can't help it. I just hug her to me and lift her off her feet. "Thanks for always being my safe person."

"Until the day I die," she confirms.

And then we're surrounded by family. The girls all want to ooh and ahh over Remi's ring, even though they've seen it before.

"I'm going to start breakfast," Gram says with a wink to me. "Let's get out of this cold. Who wants pancakes?"

"Me," the boys reply, raising their hands and scurrying after Gram.

Remi and I are the last to walk inside. "You're sure you want to sign on for this craziness?"

"Are you kidding? This is the adventure of a lifetime."

EPILOGUE

~REMI~

Nine Months Later

"I can't believe we're finally at the glacier." I take a sip of my water and stand next to my husband as we take it all in. It's damn windy up here, and there are critters I've never seen before, but the scenery is just to die for. "Look at those rock formations."

"Glaciers do incredible things to the landscape," he agrees and chews on his protein bar. "It's a great day for it."

"I'm glad we waited until later in the season." I watch as a white mountain goat picks his way along the side of a cliff. "It's the end of August, and it's still cold up here."

"It's never hot up here. Not really." Seth wraps his arm around my shoulders and gives me a squeeze. "Besides, we were busy planning a wedding, and the ranch was crazy this summer."

"I love that we got married out by the tree." I smile up at him. "With all of those hearts and initials nearby. Your mom and Cara spent *hours* hanging flowers from the branches, and your dad insisted that he should mow the field."

"They all worked their asses off," he says with a nod. "It went off without a hitch. Because you planned it perfectly."

"I'm a planner," I remind him with a laugh. "So, if we kept going that way, where would we end up?"

He spends the next twenty minutes explaining what connects where in the park. I've learned that although Glacier National Park is big, the trails connect in all kinds of crazy ways.

If you want to hike more than twenty miles, that is.

And there was a time that I would have jumped at the chance.

But something tells me that this will be my last hiking season for a while.

"I have news," I say before we start back down to the chalet, where we decided to spend the night.

"Oh?" He raises a brow. "What's up?"

"Well, there's going to be a new King in the family in about seven months."

He blinks, and then his eyes drop to my stomach. "You're pregnant?"

"Yep."

"For sure this time?"

"Yes, you idiot." I laugh as he picks me up in a hug and twirls me around.

"Wait, why did we hike up here? That's too much, Rem."

"My doctor said it was okay. Really."

"Okay, if Hannah said it was safe, I guess it's all right. But this is it."

I grin. "I thought you'd say that. I'm okay with shorter hikes. I'm pregnant, Seth, not disabled. I just won't overdo it."

He takes my hand and pulls me to him. Kisses me. "I love you, Rem."

"I love you, too, handsome. You're gonna be a daddy."

His skin goes a little green, and I smile.

"Don't worry, it'll be fun. An adventure."

"Right." He nods slowly. "And we have help."

"*So* much help," I agree. "We can't screw this up."

His face softens. "Can we name it Jeffrey if it's a boy?"

"I like that. What if it's a girl?"

He chews on his lip and looks out over the glacier before us. "Would you be upset if I suggested Carolina? Maybe we can call her Lina for short so we don't confuse the two of them."

"I'd have been surprised if you didn't suggest it." I link our fingers and lean on his biceps as we watch an eagle soar above the valley below, then take a deep breath. "It's the way it should be."

DID you love Seth's story, and want to see where it all began? You can do just that and pick up LOVING CARA, the first book in the Under the Big Sky saga!

https://www.kristenprobyauthor.com/under-the-big-sky

Do you love small town romance? Well, coming in 2022 is an all new series to love from Kristen Proby! Set in the coastal town of Huckleberry Bay, comes LIGHTHOUSE WAY, the first in an epic new series about three best friends, a local legend, and finding love on the stunning Oregon Coast!

https://www.kristenprobyauthor.com/lighthouse-way

Luna Winchester's life is firmly entrenched in the coastal town Huckleberry Bay, Oregon. A fourth-generation light keeper, Luna is carrying on the Winchester tradition by tending to the lighthouse. Plus, she's opening her new B&B, Luna's Light, on the property. Surrounded by family and her two childhood best friends, her life is full.

Wolfe Conrad is in hiding, and he's come to Huckleberry Bay to heal. A career ending accident on the track nearly took his life, and now he seeks refuge to try and build a new one. The quaint town's slowpoke rattles the man who's first love is fast cars — and then there's the beautiful innkeeper, who rattles him in different ways.

Falling in love with Luna definitely isn't part of Wolfe's plan. Local legends that tell of unrequited love and despair? Unbelievable. But stranger things have happened, like two strangers falling in love...

ABOUT THE AUTHOR

Kristen Proby has published more than sixty titles, many of which have hit the USA Today, New York Times and Wall Street Journal Bestsellers lists.

Kristen and her husband, John, make their home in her hometown of Whitefish, Montana with their two cats and dog.

facebook.com/booksbykristenproby

instagram.com/kristenproby

bookbub.com/profile/kristen-proby

goodreads.com/kristenproby

NEWSLETTER SIGN UP

I hope you enjoyed reading this story as much as I enjoyed writing it! For upcoming book news, be sure to join my newsletter! I promise I will only send you news-filled mail, and none of the spam. You can sign up here:

https://mailchi.mp/kristenproby.com/newsletter-sign-up

ALSO BY KRISTEN PROBY:

Dream With Me
You Belong With Me
Imagine With Me
Shine With Me
Escape With Me
Flirt With Me
Change With Me

Check out the full series here: https://www.
kristenprobyauthor.com/with-me-in-seattle

The Big Sky Universe

Love Under the Big Sky
Loving Cara
Seducing Lauren
Falling for Jillian
Saving Grace

The Big Sky
Charming Hannah
Kissing Jenna
Waiting for Willa
Soaring With Fallon

Big Sky Royal
Enchanting Sebastian
Enticing Liam
Taunting Callum

Heroes of Big Sky

Honor

Courage

Shelter

Check out the full Big Sky universe here: https://
www.kristenprobyauthor.com/under-the-big-sky

Bayou Magic

Shadows

Spells

Serendipity

Check out the full series here: https://www.
kristenprobyauthor.com/bayou-magic

The Romancing Manhattan Series

All the Way

All it Takes

After All

Check out the full series here: https://www.
kristenprobyauthor.com/romancing-manhattan

The Boudreaux Series

Easy Love

Easy Charm

Easy Melody

Easy Kisses

Easy Magic

Easy Fortune

Easy Nights

Check out the full series here: https://www.
kristenprobyauthor.com/boudreaux

The Fusion Series

Listen to Me

Close to You

Blush for Me

The Beauty of Us

Savor You

Check out the full series here: https://www.
kristenprobyauthor.com/fusion

From 1001 Dark Nights

Easy With You

Easy For Keeps

No Reservations

Tempting Brooke

Wonder With Me

Shine With Me

Kristen Proby's Crossover Collection

Soaring with Fallon, A Big Sky Novel

Wicked Force: A Wicked Horse Vegas/Big Sky Novella
By Sawyer Bennett

All Stars Fall: A Seaside Pictures/Big Sky Novella
By Rachel Van Dyken

Hold On: A Play On/Big Sky Novella
By Samantha Young

Worth Fighting For: A Warrior Fight Club/Big Sky
Novella
By Laura Kaye

Crazy Imperfect Love: A Dirty Dicks/Big Sky Novella
By K.L. Grayson

Nothing Without You: A Forever Yours/Big Sky
Novella
By Monica Murphy

Check out the entire Crossover Collection here:
https://www.kristenprobyauthor.com/kristen-proby-crossover-collection

Made in the USA
Coppell, TX
13 December 2021

68355914R00152